McX

by the same author

Fisher's Hornpipe

McX

A Romance of the Dour

Todd McEwen

Secker & Warburg
London

First published in Great Britain 1990
by Martin Secker & Warburg Limited
Michelin House, 81 Fulham Road, London SW3 6RB

A CIP catalogue record for this book
is available from the British Library
ISBN 0 436 27024 2

Printed in Great Britain
by St Edmundsbury Press Ltd, Bury St Edmunds
and bound by Hunter & Foulis Ltd, Edinburgh

CASSIUS W. McEWEN
JOHN REGINALD MURRAY

Little know you of the hearts
I have hidden here.

Hogg

I

THE COMPLAINT
OF SCOTLAND

For I prophecy that the English will recover their horns the first.

Christopher Smart

AULD LICHT

Consider a long and famous river, it teems with salmon and story. Winds majestic through the most various of Scotland's shires. Where it passes under several bridges and reflects a suggestion of Georgian elegance, sad tales begin.

Stand on the railway bridge until you tire of the cold and noise and the smell of diesel. Walk down the Marketgate, the Nethergate, through a damp little close, on to the wet ankle-twisting stones of the Nevernevergate. Follow along to the Auld Licht and open the vestibule door

to find McX, peripatetic inspector of ¼ and ⅕ gills (and as such a servant of Her Majesty) gored and bleeding on the horns of his nightly dilemma: lounge or public?

The round shoulders of McX become rounder as he broods, shifting from one hoof to the other like a ruminant, on concepts of the lounge: the lads in skew-fitting professional clothing, suits made from the upholstery of their company cars. Cocktails, an absurd pretension of the Auld Licht; giddy secretaries. Talk of sport among the young men becomes slackjawed, lewd. Talk of mortgages gives way to back-stabbing and vicious mating talk. Video game, jukebox – they would all start screaming.

McX rushes to the door of the public and pulls with all his might.

Camaraderie is forced on men. They have little else in life. Forced especially on the desperate, the unimaginative, who must drink the same drink in the same place every day.

How to be alone in the midst of fellowship? One can turn the other stool, try to indicate with the shoulder one wants privacy. One can snap like a little animal. But this breeds suspicion. In the end you're never left alone.

But neither does camaraderie really exist. It is a creation of racists and war-novelists. Rather, there is an *erotism* about men drinking together.

Come. Come, you must come with us into our happy love cloud. A public bar is the boudoir of a comic-opera seductress: bulbous atomisers, weird musks, pink flounces. You're dragged in, into it. Resistance will yield only remorse and confusion.

Now here in the Auld Licht, grey light from blinds. 'Scottish Literature', BBC1: watery eyes of old men turn from pipes and pints and the *Daily Star* to see Robert Louis Stevenson, a child actor. Candlesticks, a stair-tower, phony coughing, his nightie...! Embarrassed looks back and forth, unease in the corners. Pint of special! Heavy broad youths guard the island behind the bar. Treasure Island, packed with fags, stacks of matches, crowned with rich bottles of demerara: voluptuous tropical breasts thrusting in the fluorescent reek.

The Auld Licht has something of the air of a mausoleum, to which its immemorial granite exterior contributes. You might peer through the immense keyhole of the outer door and see catafalques dimly lit from clerestory windows. It is well known that the Auld Licht is neither more nor less clean and happy a place than the typical Victorian family vault.

And there is something wheat-sheaf and classical urn about McX's needs of the place. He is one of those who covet bar paraphernalia. At home he amasses beer-mats, bar-towels, ash-trays and match holders, for his soul, his McKa, to take into the next world. McX's behaviour in the Auld Licht is Egyptian. Mummy-like he stands, hands close to his chest, cigarette and pint his crook and flail.

Money is needed in the afterlife. The wooden architrave above the bottles is papered with strange money. Here McX's eyes often take refuge when he can bear no longer any other aspect of the Auld Licht:

An angry Oriental in the uniform of a western general rules a small blue note from behind giant horn-rimmed spectacles. An African with metal coils on his neck and discs in his lips stares at McX. On a note to the value of TIU KROWERIUJ, Florence Nightingale and Gandhi

face each other across a field of burning
hayricks. What a couple. Although she might
have appreciated the diaper.

All the little nations which fell over themselves to portray our lovely Queen! On some of
these bills she looks frightened, on others ferocious, on still others she looks like a man.

Creased dark little offerings from the Scottish
banks of long ago. The Linen Bank. The
Distillers Bank: finely engraved clouds scud
over the Forth Rail Bridge. The Governor and
Directors of the Boiled Beef and Carrots Bank
promise to pay the bearer . . .

Small, steel-strong American dollars: com-
mandos creeping through the play-money
jungle of the world. How many of these absurd
currencies depend on them, how many econo-
mies the American economy?

What to do in a mausoleum, a temple? If you
are not the occupant, you perform rituals.

There is a ritual way you order the life you
lead at your rented half-metre of bar. In this
rectangle of pleasure your cigarettes and your
lighter must be neatly arranged, their edges
parallel to the bar-towel, if you are fortunate
enough to have one. Your glass must be clean
and cool. Three cigarettes must pose out of the
packet at differing lengths as they do in commercial advertisement.

See, this is your real home, here in the rect-angle of pleasure. Here everything serves YOU, and you rejoice you can pay for it. Every-thing is neatly *arranged* and you can light your pals' cigarettes with florid gestures you learned from American television. Everything is neat and you can pantomime these small elegances even though your fingernails are dirty and you haven't washed your hair in days.

Ritual second: the out-of-the-blue wheezing out of *Och Aye* when you are settled with pint and dram and have arranged properly the rectangle of pleasure. Cigarette lit, you stare wonderingly up through the mirk at the stars that haunt the ceilings of all public houses.

In the rear of the mausoleum is located a small water temple. On entering you are struck with the stark, almost Japanese beauty of the bare walls, the serious light sedulously pro-vided by the frosted window-glass, by the strong odour of humanity at its most vulner-able. The floor is of two thick marble slabs, an inch above the surrounding trough, awash in ? some mixture of aqueducted and human liquids. In winter a fine mist rises from the floor.

The damp sterile quiet is inspirational, again, reminiscent of the Japanese tea-house, though the nectars here are drunk only by the mighty municipal drain. If only that hardy piece of pig-iron could tell its story!

Here is the tomb of men's wish to ignore the Devil's clamour from their fleshy little taps.

McX raises his glass. Not in a festive way. He raises his glass but instead of drinking from it he looks through the 80/- at the enoranged gaggle of buddies. They are all there. As usual they are all there. They are there there there, whether McX looks at them through his pint or not, whether he looks at them through his dram or not, whether he looks at them or not, they are there. As usual.

OF McX

In all the world McX has only two *mannerisms*. They are: to drag deeply on his cigarette and squint at someone or something as he blows smoke out of himself; and to nod, slowly, as if commiserating, at anyone speaking on any topic. Even if they are telling a joke, they get sympathy, which often angers them.

McX also has a *jest.* He occasionally mis-pronounces or *hyper*-pronounces things with his Fife accent. Example: *Liverpuil.* No one kens what he's talking about and they don't find this funny.

And McX has an *attitude* he strikes: he prides himself on the amount of applied knowledge he has on various subjects: tobacco, brewing, postage stamps and, as a sop to the working man, St Johnstone FC. In the particulars of all this information he is dead wrong.

McX is always on the verge of complete physical breakdown or complete self-rehabilitation and rejuvenation. Think of him standing in front of the swimming baths, smoking, squinting at the ticket man inside the front door, looking as if someone is shining a bright light on him.

I must get back to my swimming, he says.

McX is five foot five. If you gave him a dose of muscle-relaxant he might come out an inch or two longer on the examining table, for he stoops, *from the neck,* the swooping stoop of dromedaries. He is not hump-backed – he has the look of someone frightened of what is going on to the rear.

Comparison with the artiodactyls is also invited by the perennial suit of McX. His profession requires it. He hides from men in the ugliest most ill-fitting clothing available. He has several suits. They are all the same. And owing to his spending his working hours in public houses, they stink.

Because of the awful nature of his suit, McX feels out of place wherever he is. He squirms and folds and unfolds so much, everyone stares at him. So much for the supposed anonymity of the suit. Perpetually McX feels cold. He never removes his jacket.

McX is always slightly bent in the middle because of a secret fear. A prolonged anxiety that one's genital is somehow on parade can lead to the most horrible imaginings and wholesale breakdown. The good tailor is the psychiatrist's friend: off-the-peg trousers breed neurosis.

It is possible that McX's peculiar posture is the result of his knowledge that he was born in Fife. When he is silent, and smokes, and squints, he is considering this dubious legacy. *Lowlander.*

There is something suffocating, something face-pushing about Fife. Despite its generous sky and loamy fields, it feels poor, passed-over. Its people have turnipy noses, thick eyelids, thicker speech, the thickest skulls in Scotland, and they smoke like chimneys. The whole place is large and breezy, yet it smells like a bar bereft of an extractor fan.

Imagine the young McX, a ghastly picture: a miniature adult, already stooped, simply *standing* on a kerb, smoking, staring at the blank dirty windows and pebble-dash of his house.

To place him in Dunfermline might be cruel, but like much of cruelty it might be true.

The Fife accent of McX: *a pocket o fogs.*

Fife is a sentimental sewer. That is perhaps what they get for holding themselves above the rest of us. Their Kingdom! Plastic Scotties from Hong Kong sell to Scotsmen in Fife.

Once McX stepped into a music shop where a man in a gold lamé jacket and a Hunting Stewart tie, his stage name Benny Glow, was demonstrating electric organs. McX, fascinated by the BAGPIPE stop, burst into tears at this English bastard's rendition of 'Grannie's Hieland Hame'.

I'm sorry, he later choked to the buddies of the Auld Licht, I don't mean to embarrass you. It's been some day.

McX wears a beard. This gingerish thing is so mollycoddled by McX that McDram thinks his balls are hiding under it. It was grown in adoration of Cameron Lunzie.

Cameron Lunzie is an acromegalic singer of the pseudonationalist ballad. He is everything McX is not: tall, strong, handsome, rich-voiced, and worry is unknown to him. McX has swollen with pride once or twice to exchange a few words with Lunzie.

That's a grand song, said McX, the one about everyone dyin.

Hae a dram! boomed Lunzie. He slapped McX on the dromedary and knocked him down.

McX's beard is the wrong shape for his body. It makes him look like a fire hydrant or some other thing of cast iron. But he thinks it makes him look traditional. Tradition is McX's weapon against the vacuumed cars and gardening catalogues of his fellow workers. McX keeps alive the balladic tradition – sensitively, alone, in his bath. He croaks out Lunzie's songs, learnt from nicotine-coated discs, looking at himself in the mirror, puffing on a cigarette.

If you don't mind my asking, said McX, do you smoke cigarettes to give your voice that extra plooman's edge?

Never touch 'em, mate! bellowed Lunzie, *kill you like a bullet!*

I must get back to my pipe, said McX.

McX had two friends, but they died. *Somhairle Mac Ille Dubh,* rotund non-worker, spent the last five years of his life before his television and a cracked plate, across which passed thousands of digestive biscuits. This way of life turned him into an albino. The doctor confirmed Mac Ille Dubh had lost all the rod cells in his eyes. He died a lingering death of gross constipation and the boredom attendant.

Kyehouse, assurance representative. The nature of Kyehouse's destruction (all these people are destroyed) was a peculiar obsession with the upper-middle classes, of which Kyehouse definitely was not a member. Kyehouse learned Received Pronunciation from a set of gramophone records and bought a blue jacket. He was a great rubberneck and constantly forsook McX to chat up some solicitor and wife at the bar. Kyehouse visited only country public houses which described themselves as 'hostelries' and looked English and served frozen trout at £18 a time. Died from this.

But frozen fish is all right with McX. His digestion is wrecked by worry. He has nightmares about, among a hundred things, chicken bhuna. The bedchamber of McX rings at night with great moans and shoutings. His every dream is a nightmare.

When is a life not a story? When it is a joke.

AULD LICHT

The blonde, composed mainly of teat and crimson lipstick, is bursting out of an affair of turnbuckles and rawhide straps. Her qualifications may only be guessed, as the great part of her is covered with little bags of nuts.

Give us a bag of nuts, says McPint.

He is in love with this blonde. For several days has been drinking her health, seducing, disrobing her, removing her chaste covering of nuts. Savouring her. McPint hates nuts but he aches for this woman, for a kiss of her, a go of her, in her contraption.

He was deeply in love with her predecessor, a thong-clad jungle maiden who prowled a tropic pool. McPint had munched himself halfway through her downfall when to his disgust an old woman blundered into the Auld Licht and purchased many bags of nuts for a group of children who bawled outside. In an instant all of his Rider Haggard beauty was revealed to McPint. He was furious.

You bloody stupid old cow!

Shut your mou you drunken horror, replied the old lady, I've a right to buy nuts.

Och, you've ruined it, ruined it for me, said McPint.

McPint suffers horribly at stool, from the nuts, but now the more or less conventional charms of this Sadeian beauty are coming clear, his appetite for them grows even stronger. He studies McX, sidelong. He feels in his pocket, weighing the budget.

McX feels the red eyes of McPint upon him. He hunches over his pint and dram, he considers drawing the bar-towel up to his chin like a blanket.

Now look at that would you, says McPint. Wouldnae ye like tae get yer Muckle Flugga intae her Sma' Glen?

McX dares not to move.

Aye ye would, says McPint, and yer Gorbals intae her Inner Hebrides, yer Craigenputtock intae her Holy Loch, yer Mons Meg intae her Out Skerries, yer Cairnpapple between her Beattocks. Eh?

McX smokes and squints.

Yer Stac Lee in her Burntisland? Have some nuts, says McPint.

No.

On me.

No thank you.

A bag of nuts! McPint calls out.

The barman Knox assaults the blonde. McPint wrestles with the sealed bag. He has to bite it.

We'll share them, man.

He pushes the bag at McX and turns back to the love of his life, a further 9cm^2 disrobed.

Och, now you're talking! Look at her! I wouldnae mind crossing ma Bonar Bridge tae get a look at her Altnaharrie.

McDram giggles chestily from the snooker table where he lies on his face.

Eh! Would you now! says McPint, turning round, searching for agreement.

McX does not want to move his body, for fear it will further excite McPint. He remains in an attitude of willed hibernation.

Knox has never spoken.

McPint is the only moving thing in the Auld Licht as he turns a load of nuts and 80/- into a slurry in his maw. The air is cold and stale. Things smoke.

McPint's glass is only barely depleted, but he begins to wonder if he has enough money for another, as well as for another bag of nuts. So as to reveal completely the perverse charms of Bambi.

He has so named her.

While McPint slithers in the Turkish bath of his desire, McX grapples with sorrow. The lumps on the outside of his jacket are not his shoulders, but the signs of inner struggle. Inside him his soul is throwing punches and the dents remain.

Dark is the day. Knox has no need of lantern light. Silence. Outside, wind: the mists of the past.

What you doing in here anyway? says McPint.

McX's sorrow has made an area of low

pressure within him. He feels he must speak, even if it is to McPint.

I am about to go on holiday.

Oh? Where you off to?

No place special.

There's an idea, pint of special! calls McPint. And a bag of nuts!

I don't want any, says McX.

Nonsense, it's yer *hols*, man. And I want to see a bit more of that.

Do you think of nothing but?

Why bother? says McPint. It all comes down to that. All. Yer health.

McPint insists his every glass be left empty in front of him. The score: glasses 8, McPint 0.

To hell, thinks McX. He drinks. He lights up. He wheezes out Och Aye. McPint crunches and slurps.

McX reflects he is giving up smoking. The way to do it: limit not your cigarettes but your matches. Aye. Matches are the thing. McX's McKa knows matches inside out.

McX asks for two brands of matches. He takes the one brand out of the one box and puts them in the other, and the reverse. Now he pats them. McPint flushes.

What you doin that for? he growls.

The Gander strike better on the Locomotive box, says McX, and vice-versa.

I've no time for activities of that nature, spits McPint.

He has been sitting in the Auld Licht for three

hours and has smoked twenty-five cigarettes. Yet he speaks thus.

I must get back to my pipe, says McX.

He thinks: he is giving up smoking by limiting his matches. Though this morning he stopped to accept a light from the torch of a welder crawling in the sewer. He is smoking more than ever. But he has reduced his match budget to twelve pence per week.

Och well, it's something.

He lives in the 1980s; he worries about his health. The best thing is destroy it and be done.

SONG OF MACKENZIE

Divers weights and divers measures, both of them are alike abomination to the Lord.

Of all the men of weight and measure celebrated in McX's department, the name MacKenzie rings loudest and most true. A tall and handsome man, MacKenzie had the rarest gift a gauger may possess: the capacity of his oesophagus was exactly ¼ gill Crown measure.

MacKenzie was a legend in the department and the county for more than fifty years. The most secretive mean landlord in the smallest most nameless village was not safe from the prying eyes and throat, the rugged marching feet of MacKenzie. On a dark day he would come storming across the moors, a lone figure, heralded by pipes of the mind – the pipes are the music of fear.

In the grave-like silence of a battered bar on a dark day, when it would seem safest to water the water of life or to put a penny in the bottom of the measure – who would know? Your solitary wrinkled and Navy Cut-smoked haddock of a customer? – here would come Mac-Kenzie, first seen as a black stick on a hill. Then the doorknob would rattle and MacKenzie would be shaking the snow or muck off his boots, making himself red in the face with blowing on his hands and with forced hearty greetings.

Aye then, Donald, it's been a time since I've seen you.

Aye Mr MacKenzie, and welcome.

All the landlords and barmen of our county called him mister. And did welcome him in a sort of a way: to be on MacKenzie's good side was to be in the grace of Scottish God, and it was not somehow possible to be put in the Lord's graces by the other gaugers, weedy wee men with bad-fitting spectacles and their clinical cases. Marching in from the wind and rain with only his gnarled and rooty stick, which looked like something that had grown on his face in the night, MacKenzie would face the bar and its customers as might the archangel Raphael.

A dram!

With trembling hands the barman, thinking of all the crooked barmen of the world and all the crooked landlords, remembrance of all the sin of history running through him, would pour out a dram for MacKenzie, knowing it was too late to remove the penny if there was one.

Hardly bothering to candle the glass, MacKenzie would heft it slightly in his hand, as if he could tell the specific gravity from the weight of it. Then he would neatly and seriously drink, not stopping to taste. This was business after all. A bulge would appear in his neck. His marvellous anatomy was gauging the drink. The slightest bit of air or the slightest excess of whisky would make him grimace. Death to the landlord who thought to curry favour by pouring too much – this too an iniquitous crime in our land. But if the measure were true, down the whisky would go with a job-well-done smile and a nod from MacKenzie. What a feeling of salvation would overcome the barman.

Gin! Vodka! Rum! in succession, the wondrous throat of MacKenzie measuring, in humble service to our Queen's dicta.

Well – he couldn't very well spit them out again could he? The laws of hygiene and common sense forbid even thinking about it.

In Scotland we drink quarter gills, quarter gills is what we like. But along after the war some money-grubbing English bastards came, with the idea of ⅕ gills. And with this MacKenzie was sunk. He had no way of altering the size of his oesophagus, and so was condemned to carry a measure with him from then on. This demoralized but did not break him, although as more and younger men came into the department he was able to specialize in danker more out of the way quarter-gill places. It was a strange sight to see MacKenzie with a measure in his hand, he hardly ever got the hang of pouring the barman's glass into it. But wasn't he the proud man – there was duty to be done.

And if you gave short measure? God help you. As the liquor went down into MacKenzie's stomach, he would turn on you a look so withering, so damning that several barmen fainted on the spot in the course of his career. Many of the others became alcoholics, if they weren't already, or ended up as suicides. MacKenzie would look about him at the other drinkers, and in a deep whisper render the verdict:

I curse this place, I close it.

If the establishment survived its official penalty, it still had to bear for months the opprobrium of MacKenzie, who would visit it only in disgust and rage. The law might have forgiven those who sought to profit immorally from the needs of their countrymen, but MacKenzie could not. Like Scotland's oil, like her rivers, her whisky was in the hands of the insane, meted out like a favour – O MacKenzie believed that all right. But if that were the system, it must be adhered to, to avoid the possibility of *all* their rights to it being taken away.

The Scots are reviled by their Celtic brothers for their precision, which amounts to compulsion. The trains of Scotland run *on time* over painstakingly parallel tracks and excruciatingly engineered bridges. Or at least they *think* they do. The clock, the machine, the perfect word – even if it is a long and clumsy one – these are the Scottish materials of the world. The exact measurement of every aspect of life is necessary to the Scots, who look down on the dreamy poets of Wales with condescension and the crazed dirt of the Irish with horror.

There would be nothing more Scottish in the world than the face of MacKenzie examining a dram. To McX measurement is but a job, and a tiresome one. To MacKenzie it is duty, from on high. Thou shalt not have in thine house divers measures, a great and a small: but thou shalt have a perfect and just weight, a perfect and just measure shalt thou have: that thy days may be lengthened in the land which the Lord thy God giveth thee.

MacKenzie was senior gauger when McX joined the department, and was his trainer and mentor. MacKenzie thought he saw in the thick neck of McX a protégé, but after several weeks it became apparent that McX's throat was not right. He found it difficult to keep liquor in the middle bit without choking, once a beer man always a beer man. So when they went about together, it soon developed that McX was the more despised, standing silently by MacKenzie with his little black case. MacKenzie found this embarrassing, as if McX were a check on his integrity.

McX could not have been a MacKenzie even if his throat were right – after drinking a quarter gill each of whisky, vodka, gin and rum, McX would fall down. He has never seen MacKenzie drunk; at the end of a day, during which MacKenzie might have had ten drams of each liquor, he would look soberly up from his typewriter, on which he was reporting direct to Scottish God on the bars he had inspected, and with a wee smile say:

How about going somewhere for a dram?

For his after-hours drink (ever only one) MacKenzie left the whisky in his mouth a wee bit, and swallowed it as carefully as he did on duty. Once in a while his eyes would widen slightly, and he would mention the town where he was born. Only mention it, with a sigh; he had finished his drink and there was nothing more to be said. Off he would go, with his stick and his Inverness cape, to the several rooms he rented above a chemist's in the town. The chemist respected MacKenzie, thought him a sober man, something like himself, and did not know his tenant was a destroying angel.

McX lives on Allotment Street. Occasionally he is vaguely unsettled by the bureaucratic pity of this name. His home is neither cottage nor house, villa nor bungalow. Neither is it located precisely in town nor in the country-side. It seems to be, in itself, and in its location, on the periphery of everything. And so its occupant.

Decorative turnips. A chill as of autumn. McX makes his way toward the road. He stands in a recess of hedge, by long tradition the bus-waiting-for place of the indigenous.

From the hedge emerges Morrison, embar-rassed at having to speak in so private a place.

Chilly the day.

Aye.

Exhaustion of the man Morrison's capacity for intercourse. General relief.

Along the bottom of the hedge, a show of all the rubbish of Scotland: crisp wrappers, beer tins, pilchard tins, torn tickets, swords, plaidies, broken bagpipes, whisky bottles, promises, armour, pockets o fogs, ships, covenants, dis-carded turrets.

McX searches in his corduroy. The crumby pocket. The air cool and so still. The smoke of McX's cigarette clings round him, a grey bag. Morrison shifts from side to side but turns out no to be wantin one.

The bus looms, looking as it does in its own advertisements and handbills. *Rolling up. Streamlining along to joy.* Its outrageous front

in distorted perspective. Merry destination in-
dicator. The geometry is mad: this bus arrives
from the realm of the four-colour map theorem.
To board this bus might mean a two-
dimensional life among the stick figures of the
yellow pages: a life of worthy intentions and
snappy service enshrined in uniforms and
earnest graphic art. Brisk wee mannies selling
you tickets. *Thanking you!*

But these are the fears of madmen! Of dafties!
Not of McX or Morrison. How else get to town?

But McX should have guessed: Exact Fare
Only. Wait Until The Bus Stops. Mind Your
Head. Stand Back Of White Line. Safe. Reliable.
Courteous. Your Driver: McOcalypse.

McX shudders as he puts his coin in the box.
McOcalypse! This bodes sore ill for the day, the
week, the month – for the rest of McX's life if
there is to be any.

McOcalypse: how describe this Culloden of a
face? To look at McOcalypse is to lose all hope.
History seems to end. Through the furrows of
his eroded physiognomy has run all human
struggle. Across it the flowers of the forest have
all wede awa. McOcalypse is the Cerberus of
the town, constantly circling it, barking in his
motor stage. His face is a long grey shovel,
caked with the dirt of graves, his teeth raped
tombs. His nose dead tissue as is his hair. From
the lashless horizons above portmanteau eye-
bags dawn twin dying stars of blistering historical anger.

McX is unable to take his seat, he is frozen in contemplation of McOcalypse. His only thought:
Out.

McOcalypse crashes the door to and starts the bus with a jolt.

Eh, says McX, em –

Well? thunders McOcalypse, his voice echoing through all the columbaria of time, scoured raw with cigarette smoke and unutterable whiskies.

I'm wondering if you can set me down at Dog Vennel, says McX.

He must be out of his mind. He is asking *McOcalypse* to stop three streets before the *accepted*... this is perverted, positively anti-Scottish; how unaccording to timetable.

McOcalypse looks at McX as though he has just come upon Our Lady chewed by sharks. He grinds tooth and gear, lurch of bus around bend. He stares ahead into the depths of infinite punishment, he groans, shrieks volcanically:

Some people think this is a bloody taxi service.

McX's kidneys feel like stone. He does not know what to do, he stands helpless as he is shot across space and time. They pass a field. Some men are in it, trying to extract something, anything from the hard earth, with the aid of a machine: some sign the planet lives. If only McX could attract their attention – smash the glass door – bloodied handkerchief waving.

McOcalypse sees McX is not going to sit down. He drives more furiously, old mannies in the rear cry oot as the bus careers from side to side –

But. Although McOcalypse is the crucible of despair and the horror of existence he is, in the end, A Scotsman. Although it is his Satanic duty to terrify McX and all passengers, neither can he bring himself to refuse his request. McOcalypse is afraid of the bus company and the public: no Scotsman wants an argument unless it is of his own making. So despite being taken to the threshold of this life, McX is set down at Dog Vennel.

O LITTLE TOWN OF NO MAYHEM

How still thy greenswards lie.

You should take a bit of UNREST with your view, a little venery with your scenery; *prefer* to find the indigent squatting in the bushes of the manicured park. Beauty is only in the completeness of the world.

Scotland is beautiful because it *is* complete. Its plainer, more English forests and glens are threatened with angry scarps, curtained with violent storms. Its savage granite lands are brushed with the spectrum complete and sparkle with some of the most delicate flowers on earth.

This, our little town, is surrounded by beauty;

at first sight the town might be thought beautiful (or elegant, a sad second). But it isn't.

Garden walls of houses fronting on the park,
topped with iron spikes and barbed wire, but
interrupted and thus made purposeless by
pretty little gates: that says it.

Here men love their gardens more than each
other, and circumvallate them so as to love
them, violently, to pieces, in private.

Morning mist is on the river and here glides
the town swan, a big tough nasty piece of work
who'll go for your groin if you're not careful.

Of all the failings of people, the most aston-
ishing and enraging is incuriosity. This town
doesn't want to know you, or me, or anything
but what is already here, in the neat flower
beds, in nice plastic bags in the shops. Nor will
it want *us* to know *it.*

The place is crawling with taboos. You can
smell them. Everyone is bent over under the
weight of 'em. Little rouged lavender-watered
town.

Conversation between Smillie, newsagent, and
Mrs McPint. Ah, so there is a Mrs McPint.

Have you no more *Daily Express*?

Och, I'm terribly sorry Mrs McPint, I've no
more at all. There's been lots of strangers in
this morning.

Strangers! [Fiddles nervously with hankie.]

Aye, there's a meeting at the city halls.

What am I going to do?

I've the *Mail.*

That's *no use at all.*

Aye.

Well I'll just have the *People's Friend* and a bag of my chocs please Mr Smillie.

Right, Mrs McPint!

Smillie busies himself doing nothing with tremendous show, in the genetic way of shop-keepers. Mrs McPint stares, abstracted, at the upper shelf of periodicals. On the cover of *Wow* a wan brunette wrapped in tin foil parts her clogged lips and bares her teeth in horrific invite. Mrs McPint shudders: the idea of McPint has burst upon her.

The town is full of scurry and unbusiness. McX rolls his shoulders up the High Street. Here is fear: there is no actual press of people, but their fears are so great and their preoccupations so complex that these invisible things bump you about just as a junk-laden crowd might.

Only a few souls dare look at you. Most walk pointedly round, rotated 180° away, a wide berth of ritual terror. Some of the bent-over ones would crack their skeletons avoiding your eyes – but suddenly – they crane their faces up at you when you come abreast, so they can tell the neighbour what you look like. What the hell! They're bent, decayed – they can risk it.

The shops are of two kinds. The cat-box sort, arrived ready-made from London, ready-decorated and ready-stocked, complete with raucous shop-girls and gaping youths: trousers, gramophone records.

And: the real shops. The sort where McX learned the reality of shopping, dragged around by a dislocated arm, his drunken uncle scowling: small grey shops so like their proprietors and the populace, shops *afraid of you*. Shops so terrified of custom their display windows are of wintry frosted glass, cold as their souls. The town in turn as cold as its shops.

Ask for something? Oh, *no! Nothing like that!* These little commercial mortuaries are our town in miniature.

Messages: rat trap. Whisky. Matches. Arrival of McX at ironmongery. In the bourgeois paradise of window-land, expensive fireplace tools.

MacTaggart is tall and monstrous.

Sir, he says.

His are the eyes of the uncomfortable subject of a daguerreotype. He speaks slowly through a quantity of saliva which while never pooling on the counter must go somewhere. Perhaps at night.

Although I am genuinely backward, I keep this shop on my own bat and have a thorough knowledge of its stock, announces MacTaggart.

I want a rat trap, says McX.

Glah, says MacTaggart, rooting.

He produces (tap) a dirty red sample board.

I have several varieties (tap). I have the Robert Burns, says MacTaggart (tap), I have the Mice Inn (tap).

My Sin? says McX.

I have, says MacTaggart, the Agony & Ecstasy (tap). From France I have the Little Death (tap). And from the United States of America, I have the All Squashed B'Gosh (tap tap t-tap).

Which is the dearest?

Glah, that would be the Mice Inn, beams MacTaggart, and a grand choice.

And which is the cheapest?

Hmph! The Robert Burns.

I'll have it, says McX. Best laid plans and a' that.

To even think of joking with MacTaggart – !

How many?

I've only the one rat.

They run in packs, you know.

They die tonight.

Mrs McPint walks up the street, rueful. Her attention is arrested by the sound of a fan blowing above a bakery. The idea

CREAM BUN

becomes important, overwhelming. As she nears the bakery window, where colour photographs of cream buns sit fading in the sunlight, Mrs McPint takes a deep breath, expecting to fill her nose with glory, with the aroma of the art of confectionery. Instead she gets a full lung of coal smoke: this fan exhausts not the bakery but the heating plant in the basement.

Mrs McPint coughing up her gut in the middle of the street attracts little attention. Everyone coughs, everyone smokes – they're no very well.

As she heaves, bent double, she is passed by a group of young people. The youth of our town, what a crew, what a sorry lot. Here they come, one after the other, limping like as not. What a collection of mumbles... lisps... you never heard such a pathetic racket. Not one in ten speaks clearly nor can one in twenty look you in the eye. Unwashed. Sloppy. Lame.

But what's this? They've stopped dead in their tracks, they're staring, something has *got their attention.* The cheeks of the girls burn, the boys goggle: a tall Italian girl in impeccable clothes, a lush mane of hair, is walking down the street. Gently she goes round the little hacking ball of Mrs McPint.

Where'd she come from eh?

Our disco-ettes go mad. They stamp their little feet with agitation and smooth their dirty canvas jackets. Their mouths pucker tighter round the sourness of life.

Who's she think she is anyway?

Come on, Jockie!

The boys grin, get their combs out, put their hands in their pockets, say brave things to each other.

Oo la la.

D'ye see that?

Wouldnae mind some French lessons!

Trapped between the town's damp past, the cheap cruelty of their present and the never-coming beautiful European future, Pictish Youth straggle off toward some place where glue may be sniffed in comfort.

Damp, damp, we're all so damp. We don't need firemen here, only smouldermen.

The town is so wound up in its own past, even the rubbish blowing in the street is covered with pictures of local monuments: historical rubbish is the only rubbish allowed.

Having recovered her breath, Mrs McPint puts her head down and *shops on.*

In a domed structure of doubtful classicism from the last century, it is McPint eft-fou.

Beyond the wee mannie who issued him a ticket – *Thanking you!* – in the shadows of the Natural History Room, McPint is disgusted to find the display PARASITES OF FAMOUS SCOTS. In formaldehyde to be sure. McPint presses his Maris Piper nose against the glass and, true to all he holds dear, compares lengths.

Carnegie wins, although Ruskin had a run for his money from the look of things. All around, mortified amphibians and half-rotted taxidermies glare at McPint through dusty panes, in murky green light. To be here is to be underwater, at the edge of an ocean of death, where things are beginning slowly to whiten and peel.

McPint squares his shoulders and bullies his way through unknowing and disquiet into the gallery.

In a long line of watercolours, various aspects of hills, cattle, fences and houses are explored in unseeing ways, the cute fireside ways. In these landscapes cattle have no importance. Do they never breathe nor crop but only decorate? And where is this Scotland anyway?

McPint knows nothing of the countryside. The profoundest way he has dealt with the idea of cattle is to lust after a cowgirl waitress in an Aberdeen vulgar cocktail bar. Yippie ki yi yo. But these birthday-card kye! Realizing there is nowhere to spit, McPint spits.

But in the next gallery McPint stands agape, sudden, before the works of Totemic Smith.

Here someone somehow has got into his own head, has *stolen* the moil of his personal intimate sickening thoughts, is *displaying* McPint's most garish glandular idiosyncrasies to the public!

McPint is embarrassed – worse – he's revolted, although this can't for the moment be seen under his bluff colour. Only in his heart, under his skin itself.

Night, Rose Street: beer glasses romp as in a

circus: boys: girls: clocks: huge green musical
notes: sexual organs and their 80/- oozings:
Highlanders charge whisky bottles with pikes:
big red lips and doughy little suspendered
hips. £650.00.

Night, Rose Street subsumes McPint, his jaw
clatters on the floor tiles, it's eating him alive:
his circulation develops knock, perspiration
runs all down . . .

After grasping like a man drowning at his
pockets to determine the ready availability of
money and virility, McPint rushes from the
gallery into the street. Debouches into immedi-
ate debauchery: he needs the Auld Licht like
most people need the toilet.

Mrs McPint in the arms of her lover of three
years, the proprietor of the Bengal Tandoor
Mahal. Despite his bulk he is muscular, and his
attentions are quite the thing, especially if
compared with the pretty incredible caresses of
McPint.

Balajiprasad is a considerate lover. When
they finish he brings in glasses of lager and
lime and a tray of anise seeds, hot towels and
cigarettes. They lie in bed and talk.

Aren't you glad we became lovers, Margaret
Rose?

Yes, Balajiprasad.

I remember the day so well. You ordered a

lamb pasanda to take away. I thought your skin was like the almonds. In the kitchen I held them in my hand and meditated on your body.

In fact Mrs McPint's skin is like dead lamb in the butcher's window.

Oh, go on!

No – to me you are very beautiful. You have a fine spirit.

I'm no very well – oh!

Balajiprasad is dribbling lager and lime on Mrs McPint. He wants to see if the anise seeds will adhere to her breasts. He is a playful chap is he not.

What a mess you're making!

It took several weeks for Mrs McPint to yield to the importuning of Balajiprasad. He told her he had a Discreet Very Private Apartment, away from his family, and that they should play there. Very very hot. Finally Mrs McPint went with him, after McPint had come home and yet again unzipped his flies and fallen asleep in his tattered reclining chair.

THE LITTLE TREATS OF GREAT BRITAIN

McX in the confectioner's, another shop cowering in the face of time. The jars the bottles the wrappers, the woman with lipstick on her chin and teeth. Labels as reliable in the registration of their faded colours (though newly printed) as the faded unflavours of the sweetmeats they shroud.

On these labels of old, happy Creoles gather cane to rot the remaining tooth of Scotland. Kickapoos harvesting roots give the mind to travel during moronic mastication. Vestiges of the British East Everywhere Company still entice men and women whose only common-wealth is drink, tobacco, sweeties. Frayed little things kept in Royal Wedding tea canisters.

So long ago, Britain's last imperial pleasures, the transcendental satisfaction of her socio-economic stomach. Now no Everests remain for her, no continents to railroad, no dusky people to blanch with trams, shirt fronts, boiled pud-dings. This is but the small verso of a big recto.

No life, no movement on these shores save the gently smoking lungs in the benefits queue.

After the war against fascism she turned inward, to soothe and content herself. But only in the tiny ways, with little treats, for the world was turning from her.

The sweetie, the pint, the fag. Romance book, war book. That thing you must have at the end of the day, the little reward for little labour done to little effect and for little reason. Believe it is your utmost.

Little treats – the art of arranging your fags and matches in the rectangle of pleasure. Toothy comics for gaiety, for passion bare bums on saucy seaside postcards. For history a distant glimpse of tired pageant, a weak wave from the watery Royal family.

Young men leave their wives alone with pieces of meat on Sundays. They stand in the public with pint and cigarette, colourful, casual, infinitely more tawdry than the tweed fathers and worn cardigan uncles next them.

Britain, you are a sickly child in ill-fitting Sunday clothes.

The little treat of a Malvinas victory, or destroying some Frog town with remote-controlled hooligans. The little *threats* of Great Britain.

Pine for the most industrial, most transitory of pleasures: they are all that are on offer. A way to soothe the sure and secret knowledge that standing in the pub you are no better than a wog being kicked and shouted down by some-one like you.

Though perhaps wogs were never so kicked and ordered about in Wogland than they are now in the safety of the public houses of Britain.

You did your job: the LMR, you worked the pit, all Creation told you to. You were Imperial, and safe.

Jock-in-the-Pub worked on the Kenya rail-way, he was an expert white. Daily in the Auld Licht he fondly reminisces:

What a bunch of niggers! Ye wouldnae be-lieve their laziness! Immorality! Their dirt!

O Jock, working for that Company, living for the monthly arrival of the *Scots Magazine* and

a carton of Capstans, haunting the brothels of
Nairobi – what were you, eh?

At night odd moments of quiet descend on
public houses. Then, men would cock their
heads and listen to the far-off sounds of empire.
They knew it from cigarette cards and sweetie
wrappers. They heard men and women cry out,
sometimes in pain, sometimes in hatred, sometimes astonishingly in loyalty.

If you had been to the pub (just a wee one eh)
before you saddled your corporation pony, the
headlights of your locomotives and omnibuses,
the light of your Davy lamps flickered briefly
across other shores, exotic dancers in the night.

Another pint of Pale India!

The bus, the seam your branch-line of
empire: your duty. You must function, no question. But at night a glimpse of something
unsavoury between the bars of pub – life –
music: for all this tradition, the wrapper un-
changing, there is punishment.

In bad little places one buys bad little biscuits.
In this world like finds like: crushed stale
biscuits are sold in crushed stale towns. To
stale, crushed McX, to whom they are as
cigarettes. He chain-eats them.

McX comes out of the sweetie shop with his
matches ration and a package of biscuits, which
he unwraps and eats one, two, three, four, five,
six, waiting for the decent one that never
comes. Biscuits so like life even the wrappers
aren't on straight.

AULD LICHT

McPint is welcomed by McStink to the hereditary table of McStink of that Ilk: a no man's land
of slop and smear, a desert of cigarette ash and
the carapaces of crisps. Even McPint finds it
distasteful to sit at McStink's table. McStink
keeps his ruined knees wrapped round one of
the legs of it in case – though no one could ever
conceive this wish – someone should try to take
it from him.

The iron stead of this table is adorned with
the heads of cherubim. McPint looks down at
one. His knee rests against it. He is surprised to
see that thanks to the overflow of liquids from
the table-top, the cherub's nose is running, onto his trousers: a little dribble of angelic iron
snot.

McPint begins to choke. He can think now
only of the paintings of Totemic Smith.

There's a man in my head, he wants to cry.

Evil exists. A shocking example of it is how
easily cigarette packets are opened. WHEREAS, it
is impossible to unwrap toothbrushes and
breakfast cereals, note the engineering, see
how perfectly cigarette cellophane is stripped
away, how sensually the box slides out. Note the
perfect printing, the tidiness of the little bas-

tards in their gaily coloured silo. How pristine they are, these heralds and soldiers of the world's dirtiest scandal, its sickest most painful death, the Bomb in its most convenient form.

McPint is such a heavy smoker, even his toenails are stained with nicotine. He is a Scot little squatsman. Thick and short he has no neck. A tunny-faced man full of rain, corrosive fats, nicotine, scarring 80/- and a full measure of the schizophrenia of Calvinism.

His nose was never broken but somebody gave it a wee push-in, with the thumb, when the dough of McPint was still soft in Auld Hornie's oven. McPint's speech is slug-like, thick as he. He rolls his Rs as Sisyphus his boulder.

McStink's roll-up makes a sound, a train stopping, and goes out.

This tobacco's like ma dochter, says McStink. Goes oot a lot.

Needs knockin up, says McPint.

McStink grimaces and moves off to the bar, away from the nastiness of McPint. McPint sits and steams away, hating and fearing what he has seen, himself, in the museum. Outside it has become a day of violent changes, now raining, now not. The men of the Auld Licht, drinking in turmoil, stretch out their pints and drams. You would think they were deep as oceans, the pints not the men. They stick their noses out into the rain, shake their heads, Have Another, No, On Me, Nae Use Going Oot In *That.*

These men, and all their countrymen and women, are hostages to the weather, just as their country is hostage to another and its lascivious politics. All, right or wrong, picture a shining life past, now choked like sea-birds with greed-foul oil.

McPint sits, miserable, in his own wee captivity. He is hostage to drink, to cigarettes, to the picture of an older Scotland of the Mind, to lurid imaginings; and now he is being held at knife-point by Totemic Smith.

There's a man in my head, snuffles McPint, alone.

McPint has imagined sleeping with his own daughter. He feels no guilt in this: he has lusted after so many women, real and Ben Day, that he cannot make out any sort of difference.

Och, they're all someone's daughters!

Too true. McPint lives in the disposable world, a world which does not exist but is sold to us daily aye daily. The length of his life, the pound in his pocket are to McPint as infinite as the parade of girls he crumples from magazines and having wet them puts into the fireplace. The sad pornography of infinity.

The same infinite sadness lets the Bomb exist: it is the Bomb. Until we see there is room for everything else *until* the Bomb is driven from among us, room for murder, for war over grain or oil, room for men corrupting their daughters, for the infinity-world of advertising, of cigarette-death, room for Jock-in-the-Pub and glue-sniffers and glorifiers of the military, room for bagpipe stops on organs and bad little biscuits, then we will have to have these things *forever,* as they are the Bomb in its grinning six-pack, family pak E-Z-Open naughty play-costume.

By day McPint manufactures a wee metal disc, the unimportant part of the important part of submarines. McPint by night cuddles himself in the warm drink nicotine pornography blanket of the Bomb. It takes care of all his needs, and he can't get enough of it.

Wha's tae blame? Here's tae us.

McStink returns to the ancient table of his clan with hesitation. McPint eyes McStink's mossy glass of fizzy beer with disgust.

Now this, says McStink, is what I call a fine pint. It's absolutely always the same, in tin, in bottle, or comin oot the font.

Aye, and the same comin oot yer rump, says McPint. What are ye tryin to do, work one up me?

What in hell's the matter with you the day? says McStink.

McStink's theory: McPint's heavily tufted ears are ingrown. Thick blood-orange strands coil around and around, piercing McPint's brain and strangulating it.

Och, to hell, says McPint.

He drinks half his pint of 80/- and as his hand with cigarette trembles he shuts his eyes, the lids vibrate, he recoils inwardly from the violation of his ethos by Totemic Smith. He thinks of the painting *Hand With Cigarette.*

In this painting it is the wrist that bothers him. It is an undernourished uncared-for wrist, trying to be elegant. It is a long wrist, curved awkwardly, decorated with a bracelet. The hand holds a cigarette over a table. On it are two English cocktails. At the very end of the arm is the slight black suggestion of a lacy sleeve. The wrist and table are lit from behind by a doorway in which a man is leaning as though not all conscious. One of his hands flops half way out of the pocket of his trousers.

McPint's eyelids quiver even more. He's been there, hasn't he? Has he admired that wan wrist, has he leant in the smoky door? This disturbing picture brings back to him a worry, the delay he is experiencing in receiving a catalogue of Glamour Wear for the long-suffering Mrs McPint. Whatever task he bends to, all McPint ever sees in the eye of his mind is the long-suffering Mrs McPint in graceless nylon fripperies.

McPint is getting even more fou. Though he knows the Auld Licht, he goes wrongly at first into the Ladies, mistaking the female Pict-O-Gram on the door for a man wearing a kilt. McPint remembers Scotland of Old, aye he does.

McPint lurches into the water temple. He starts to rattle at the contraceptive vending machine.

Och, this is no use!

You don't want one of those anyway, says Knox. I say it's a disgrace to name a prophylactic Fiesta.

Eh! McPint looks at Knox with contempt.

It's their national festival, says Knox. How would you like it if in Mexico they sold rubbers called St Andrew's Day or Burns Night?

Well, says McPint, after staring at Knox for a full minute, they don't.

McPINT FOU

Fou. Staggers along the street in yellow vapour. His degenerating gut precedes his disordered mind which mulls over the possibilities of sin.

Arrives at the premises of Smillie, newsagent, more particularly pornmonger, cloaked in darkness. Pushes pink and wide and snorting against the glass. Adding his hands he makes a suction-cup of his face; with a leisure unavailable during opening hours he may scan the upper shelf: *Wow, Big Ones, Yeah Baby.*

McPint ascertains the exact location of *Wow* so when Smillie opens he can rush in and grab it automatically, avoid being seen to peruse the shelf, violently fling *Wow* at the girl and have his money ready in his shaking hand. If there are others in the shop, learn to hate them:

loudly call for cigarettes, morning rolls.

Q: Smillie has a wife and daughter. Why does he sell *Wow*?

A: Smillie does a roaring trade in *Wow*. Choice is the essence of the Prime Minister's vision.

Having made a real mess of Smillie's window, McPint goes up the street. Someone may be surprised at the scum in the morning but not Smillie. Smillie is used to scum.

McPint is no well. McPint is very poor off. In the back of his mind, politeness is awash, there is some dead root of the circumspect: so McPint eschews the gutter. He totters toward the cash machine in the bank wall, manages to insert his card, the door slides up; he vomits, urgently, into the thing's flashing protesting innard.

Fair do.

Weaving toward the bus station and humming, McPint fails to distinguish a white form, dim in a doorway. It is the town swan, a feared thing and the subject of many superstitions. It goes for McPint, who succumbs to this attack, yielding easily up more of his liquid estate.

Awakens some time later and proceeds, cheery, unremembering, to the terminal.

SCOTLAND OF THE NIGHT

Sodium vapour lamps. High Streets sleep with gallons of history in them. Stale yellow light: the bus goes.

Fish and chicken bars sit riddled with the grease of asleep, the chicken eye shut and the fish eye open, dreaming of drunken snackers who did not free them but will tomorrow aye tomorrow.

Everywhere the damp smell of the last cigarette in the world. Beer dregs.

Behind the occasional dim-lit window shade, one of two things happens a thousand times in Scotland of the Night: a drunken man paws helplessly at his wife who, ignoring him, moves her lips to the rhythm of a story in a magazine. Or: living out some angry tragedy, a smouldering chair begins to consume its unconscious occupant.

If in nightmare or your cups you were to get lost in Scotland of the Night, lost in the yellow light, stumbling in streets of fish and chip granite tombs, scratching at funereal doors that will never open, would you ever find your way back to the day? Eh?

Where would be the little stair to take you back to the shores of an isle you love, ye banks and braes, or Princes Street, Edinburgh? Could you find it in the smarting yellow? In the disturbing death's wind?

The last fish and chip bus leaves the town, the driver McOcalypse. The reek of his cigarette swirls about the heads, nodding braying heads. Radio clashes with tape and tape with smell. A man rises. Again. In counterpoint to the bus's roll he rises, hooray and up he rises, battles to the rear, a desperate urge on him to open several sluices.

Sodden fish and tatties in newspapers streaming oil, the misery-thick air, the occasional sign caught in the headlamps.

There is nothing more put away from God, nothing with less to do with the world than McOcalypse's omnibus of night.

SCOTLAND, WHISKY & THE BOMB

McPint creeps along the sitting-room floor. Creeps with narrow eyes and a great craving for further oblivion. Sights, in the distance, the sideboard. Repository of Mrs McPint's tipples and laughed-at gift liqueurs, reserved for company that never comes.

On his belly McPint grapples with the little key, makes too much noise, for which thickly curses and then curses self for cursing.

McPint likes alcohol made in monasteries. Men of God don't fool about. They have good reasons to get rat-faced. But McPint yanks out: MKOJO. AFRICAN LIQUEUR. Lustily he rubs the protuberances of this exotic bottle. Uncorks, drinks deep here in the dark of MKOJO. Before half a gill of this has gone down him, McPint hears jungle drums.

Jungle drums say more drink! Aloyah! Jungle drums say white women in bin! Aloyah!

MKOJO goes down a treat. After all, its colour cannot be seen. On to several more bottles. Far from sickening McPint, these treacles heat him and bother him. They and his remembered imagination of the contents of *Wow*. A night cutie in a cute nightie.

In the bedroom the breasts of the long-suffering Mrs McPint rise and fall in slumber along with the rest of her.

The liqueurs gone, McPint crawls into the kitchen, ransacks the bin like a dog, panting, and at last finds: Fiona. All – ahh – sucked out early in the day, this priestess of lager. At breakfast? McPint popped her top and filled himself with her nectar. Now he pounds on the lid of her resting place, interrupts the slumber of this tenant of the bin to drag her out and have her. Fiona is McPint's favourite name for women he wants.

He places the empty tin on the edge of the sink: Fiona looks down on him. McPint mirth-lessly, quickly, on the moonlit kitchen floor, deep in a confused anaesthesia of desire and Mкojo. *Fiona Fiona Fiona, ma Crannogs in yer Whangie.*

McPint approaches the marital couch with trepidation, still crawling.

Now he lies beside Mrs McPint, barely able to control the ailerons of the sum of his ingestion. He is aware and afraid of her, breathing, warm, flushed; he thinks of her milkiness and her vagina. There they are, asleep.

Diaphragmatic spasm, resulting in audible and olfactory cloud.

I've been thinking, says Mrs McPint, waking up. Thatcher was on the telly.

What? says McPint.

She's needin bloody shot, says Mrs McPint.

McPint feels around in the bed. A half-empty box of chocolates, the obituary pages of several newspapers: Mrs McPint likes to torture herself by reading the little memorial poems.

> *O Grannie dear we greatly fear*
> *That sadly you are dead.*
> *You paid the price of winter ice*
> *And fell upon your head.*

He feels at last the leg of Mrs McPint or part of it.

How about a go? asks McPint, gaseous.

Ye ken, I wouldnae care if they dropped that Bomb right now, says Mrs McPint, suddenly so tired.

The hands of McPint coming toward her, across her, make her desirous of her fondest wish, annihilation. Everyone the long-suffering Mrs McPint knows in this our cold grey town is in agonies of some kind or other. We worship the hydrogen Bomb through its totems daily and we all pray it is going to come and rid us of worldly care. O the boom, the bonny bonny boom – Boom! go the Cowdenknowes.

McPint prepares to hoist himself atop Mrs McPint. He wonders if he is going to be ill. Crankily he kneads her rumpus, remembering something.

You know what I'd like? says Mrs McPint.

What eh? says McPint, surprised.

I'd really like a curry just now, says Mrs McPint, isn't that funny.

McPint passes out. Mrs McPint puts out the light and shortly sleeps, dreaming of the dark skin, the grey moustache and chest hairs of Balajiprasad, and of the atomic Bomb.

McPint's bed soars, lost, through space, beyond his budget, through the paintings of Totemic Smith: McPint's bed is filled with the pop singles, chewing gum, lipstick and pink tights of all the young girls of Caledonia.

Twice a year McX takes a holiday of nine days from the Weights and Measures. Not to expose his odd body on a beach – not even a beach of

Britain, which, grey and damp, would cradle him harmonically.

No, in his work McX has enough of travel. Moving across lines and markings he cannot see on the land but must grapple with on the map fatigues him, makes him feel old and ill. For every line of the national grid McX crosses on duty, there is another line on his face. He counts both, grid lines and crows' feet, before each holiday, gauger to the last.

No, the holiday McX takes is a holiday to the interior. First he lays in supplies: coffee, tea, cream crackers, whisky, cigarettes, biscuits, fly swatter, bodhrán, a rabbit from Cambeul the butcher (hung several weeks from a metal hook through its legs), and a number of newspapers and magazines.

Once inside his house, on holiday, McX stuffs blankets into every crevice, he draws all blinds and curtains. The arrangement of his chair and reading lamp is a precise and secret affair. Then for nine days McX sits in his chair, looks at the periodicals, eats biscuits, smokes, beats the bodhrán, sings and drinks hot drinks. But stay: there is tremendous variety in his holiday.

Sitting naked in his shroud of smoke and cracker crumbs, he travels the earth and has many adventures. He climbs mountains, cycles, conducts noted orchestras, addresses parliaments. He does lie on beaches, the National Geographic beach, and the unreally white sands of travel brochures, portions of dictatorships set aside for the spendings of white people.

His reading lamp is the sun and the moon. The smoke of his cigarette is morning mist, the pile of biscuit wrappers and fag cellophane a rustling forest floor. The Scots are great folk for the travelling, oh aye.

But travel smoking and crackers are not the epitome of McX's holiday. It is to dream, imagine new chapters in an encyclopaedic edifice of a Scotland that has been in him for years.

McX has nothing. O he has two mannerisms, a jest and an attitude, he functions all right, he walks he talks. But really he is just a thermal mass which requires a job and breakfast.

McX has no country, its sovereignty debased several hundred years ago. Corporations and the Government have taken the place of press-gangs and dukes. Scotland votes Labour and McX with her. But the tiny bugs under your kitchen sink: do you care what their *politics* are? As long as the English are happy with their greedy sloppy brand of American life, they can rule Scotland without lifting a finger.

McX has no culture. On his daily round of dreary tap rooms, people gulp and sweat either to blind themselves to the sorry vestiges of what this place was, or to drug themselves into a mad idea of what it is. Scotland's history is washing, washing her sheets, pressing them, and lying down in bed. As despair grows the sheets are washed ever furiouser, but now the sleeper is dead; there is not even a stain from her leakings. What choice does McX have but to dream his nation?

Some volumes of McX's encyclopaedia are in boats, violins sailing to Skye, in the libraries of baronial castles. On chases of song across the tops of Highland glens. Or they contain every maizy song funnelled oot the wireless to his Grannie, when McX was a sallow youth nooping over his bowl of porridge. Tartanism and tarantism.

And, he has no mate. What do you suggest for him? The barmaids, the bank clerkesses? He can squeeze an evening's talk out of his job, the pride he takes in his immensely Scottish profession – measuring things with official cylinders. Every day measuring an aspect of Scotland's bondage, the degrees of spirit allowed them as drinkers exceeding those allowed them as men.

Sometimes on holiday McX will get out his collection of ladies' handwriting: notations of his balance from Morag at the bank, PAID written in an attractive hand on the gas bill, several sweetly complaining letters stolen from the office. By covering one eye with a cracker and slowly scanning one of these letters, McX can compose, one character at a time, a love letter to himself in the woman's own hand, on the linotype of his brain.

Then he might beat the bodhrán.

But within his great and traditional unreal ism, McX is in very real love.

II

HIGH

LAND

WOMAN

I will make my kitchen, and you shall keep
   your room,
Where white flows the river and bright
   blows the broom,
And you shall wash your linen and keep
   your body white,
In rainfall at morning and dewfall at night.

            Stevenson, 'Romance'

Arises from a nightmare bed asleep? awake? in the small station hotel of smells. Arises from an unholy confluence of several of the waters of life: flowers that bleed and a brutal patricide.

Dresses, not without being taken aback by his dromedary body in the crumbling French mirror, somehow at home in the shabby room. Looks out the window into a back lane: piles of casks, a pine tree fresh and bending in the distance, beyond the wall.

Complications of the vestibule and its locks but emerges from. Looks at his corduroy shoulders in a puddle left by rain from the Highlands in the night. Walks down the road and along a high stone wall.

One of the gates is open. Steps through it, walks up an avenue of limes. There is mist – the wee mannie who makes fogs has been here.

Rectangular and conical, yet watching, sharp and hard as all of wildlife, rustling, as if breathing the mist and the leaves in and out, the castle, black and white before him. The mist surrounding is higher here, the castle perhaps its source.

Beneath the stumpy clock tower, a strip of gravel marched at dusk by a piper.

In the entrance hall, oak panels and balconies

look down. The effect, always chilling, of tartan
bunting and dark wood, armour and weapons.
Empty helms and breast-plates challenge, puf-
fed out, ready to seize the nearby pikes and
swords. A helmet without a head in it, a faceless
determined soldier. What a fright.

Heads of great deer. Greater headless antlers:
weapons too after all.

Pay the wee mannie. Here he is, his ticket
machine, the ever present reek of Err-Na-More
tobacco, the smell of wee mannies who collect
tickets and make fogs.

Thanking you!

A long hall, dim Georgian green with white
mouldings. A carpet red with soakings of blood
stretches away, ago, long back into its own
history. The hall of the land: a forest of antlers
on the walls, twenty years of the Duke's
favourite stag.

From this hall lead rooms of dream: dreams
of rooms and rooms that dream of other rooms.

Portraits on the great stair, successors to the
house. Some painted unabashed to show,
others to hide, the hereditary defect, a wall-eye,
dreaded by the commonality. A lurid light
extinguished only when the ninth Duke married a Sassenach. O drastic step.

Lace collars and india-ink backgrounds of
a varnished vanished life. Men in suits, suits
of armour, suits of velvet, suits of tartan,
suits of hide. O fellows, why do we always hide
in suits? To make more businesslike the

business of killing.

The family stare, stare down the painter, you, me, him, stare down the nose, the poverty, the wars and mists and trees, stare down armies of English and armies of tourists, stare aristocrat-ically down the bloodied Georgian hall, stare as people no longer stare. Anymore no one has the bollocks.

Goes up a turret stair. Halfway up sees a low door set into the curving wall. The glass curtained. What is behind this door that stinks of secrecy? Things too terrible for the tour. This perhaps the door to nightmare. To McPintish, though more ducal, tendency. The secret fears of all Scotland: behind this door breathes the knowledge that destiny is gnashing its teeth in a London killing-jar. In this room the women of Scotland wail and walk in a circle of mistreat-ment, cooking and step-scrubbing. The fog maker in a corner, boiling his hot-plate. This wee door may open into a tremendous hall where perished children and brave souls embalmed in alcohol are arranged in glass cases, cared for by the scrubbing polishing female ghosts: little death's head at the door with a ticket machine. Thanking you!

Does the curtain of the intriguing door lift as McX passes it? The curtain-twitching ghosts of a thousand ruined villages.

Away, and polish your already gleaming tiles as you did in life!

A curious room at the top of the turret: its view
of the glen through a narrow eight-paned
window, the steep slope of trees. Dark green
walls. A bed covered with a tartan blanket set
near a tiny coal fire, a fire so much smaller than
the fireplace in the great drawing-room only a
few steps away. The meagreness, the *past* of
this room's furnishings make it small indeed;
its sphere of light is low. It is not of the castle
but of the glens and hills and cottages outwith.

McX paints this room with the sunlight of late
autumn, bleeding orange through the window,
down on the deep green and blue and oak of
the tartan and the bed.

This is the room of his life with Siobhan, life
like the sum of wood, faded cloth and autumn
light. Just like her the softness of the small fire,
the view of the coloured hill; all in this room
are as they are in her, as they are in the stoop-
shouldered mind of McX, who is not insensible
to beauty. Especially where he may smoke as
much as he likes – cigarettes are free in his
dreams and available on every corner there.

And here is Siobhan.

She carefully tends the fire. They eat at the
scarred table: domesticity is upon them, a
bulwark against the coming winter. It is night:
moonlight blasts through the window.

McX warms between the lushness of Siobhan
and the fire. Her eyes and chestnut hair glim-
mer in the confusion of lights. For the first time
in his life, desire bids McX shed his corduroy

coat, and he is warm without it. Warm: all his skeleton, organs, skin warm. Warmth is the precious drug of Scotland.

He plummets, miles, down down into the counterpane, shuts his eyes, blissfully composes himself. Systematically to dream her completeness, ignoring her reality. This night they will spend a year in bed.

There is no desire like that to impregnate or be impregnated. If you two could take your hearts out still beating and fondly rub them together, watch 'em romp on the bed – that would make screwing look pretty pedestrian eh?

Despite the inadequacies and bafflements of their desire, this is love – they want to make a thing to love.

But all round Siobhan's bed, the blanket, the loved coal fire, the autumn light McX painted on the face of Beinn-a-Ghloe fade away. McX's dromedary form moves in sleep next her. Siobhan is surrounded by ghosts. Of brownyis and of bogillis full is her bed.

Siobhan's days are mystifying. She seems to struggle through them that she may have time properly to dread night. The interstices of her life are filled with ghosts, blue flames, thin above the coal.

A bright day, a gentle and chill breeze from the Moray Firth: summer.

How ominous sunlight can be, foreboding, playing in the leaves of the few trees of the Highlands.

She had leaned her little bicycle against the stone wall. In her dress: her grandmother always dressed her nicely. Just for a keek round the yett of the graveyard, a little game, but oh!

Just as she looked, something stopped dancing and: vanished.

Saw it was gone. Now there was only the Moray wind and the sunlight and the stones.

And the clanking chain of the little bicycle: fast, home, but not to tell. They already think her strange. She isn't wanted, she wasn't wanted, but she wants to be there now. To touch the cool cream tiles in the clean green stair instead of the warm tombs, to smell the tile polish and Sunlight rather than the wind of the Moray. To look at her doll.

O, they know ghosts in this place. Why else polish and scrub the stairs and tiles of the world but to banish loitering spirits?

They will not listen, they will not want to hear, even if they asked. Just as she does not want to hear the daily anger of her grandmother's footsteps. As she does not want to hear her grandfather knock drunkenly down his midnight table of bottle and patience, as she did not want to hear him stumble to his wife's room and in a pathos of age demand to have her. As she does not want to hear the breeze that follows, just behind her, always: the wind from the firth which blew through the clothes of that which stopped dancing and stopped being as soon as she –

But does hear. And watches. And grows, slowly, in an igneous world gone grey with history, still touched with the lack, torpor, and stupefaction of war.

Here aeroplanes flew daily off to Germany, flew through the air of Moray, flew through ghosts and brought back more. Aeroplanes then forgotten as Scotland turned back to the factory, the sweetie-shop and the pub, the grey and distant television.

Of Archie and Jean, her parents: not to dispose of them any more quickly than Hitler did, with a bomb on the Empire Cinema, Glasgow.

Their one night out on their one holiday of the war.

Because of their strained union, only the second time they made love. The first time they made Siobhan, and Jean said that was enough, and went back to smoothing her skirt full-time.

In the Empire Archie was squirmin in his seat, wonderin if he could get Jean to do it again the night. It wasnae so bad, she hadnae seemed to mind it. An it was wicked fun.

She had carefully placed her black dress over the worn armchair. Archie felt he was having an *affair*, fun, like his brother Roy the salesman.

Jean's one good black dress on the chair: light
and noise from Sauchiehall Street. She left her
stockings on, her only stockings. But it wasnae
for him. She merely wanted out of bed and
dressed as soon as he was done.

A damp feeling came over Archie, a heavy
idea that being in bed in marriage oughtn't to
feel like sin.

As Archie in the cinema wriggled and rem-
inisced, without touchin Jean or even buyin
her nothin, she watched the giant masculine
chin on the screen. She wondered if it scratched
its lovers as Archie's chin scratched her.
Whether they liked it, whether the owner of the
chin had ruined their stockings, whether they
had any; whether the chin went with girls at all.

There they sat in the Empire, distracted by
their own desires from the distraction they had
gone there for. Desires they had only twice
admitted.

On the screen, quite another Scotland was
being built for them, and brought a wee tear to
the eyes o many. Every man and woman in the
Empire was a Scot, and knew their land – yet
the Drambuie-dripping collation served them
on the screen, which they all knew never was,
made them howl with sentiment. They bellowed! This was cynical torture, shades of the
wireless – they blundered into the aisles and
fights began . . .

It is the Scotsman's daily work to make
Scotland in his mind, then see what the next

chap's come up with. It must be made fresh
every day. Baker. Confectioner. Butcher. Isn't
this what McX is doing, lying next Siobhan?
They couldn't put up with the store-bought
Scotland being ladled all over them in the
Empire. But war had weakened their defences.
So magic happens. And was happening and
many Scotlands were being made and bought
and eaten in the Empire that night, when in the
love scene a brief whirrr! was heard and:
bomb's your uncle.

Her grandparents did not encourage friends.
Nor did the white house a mile from the road,
scrubbed by her grandmother and swept by
history and the Moray wind. But Siobhan found
a friend in Rabbie.

  Pale poles for legs, thick spectacles. None the
less it's Rabbie this and Rabbie that. Grandfather, smelling of whisky, takes her to Aberdeen twice a year, to the pictures with Rabbie.
And Siobhan a picture of Scotland too, dressed
by her grandmother: hair-band, little bag (a
concession won in Woolies, grandfather drunk
and munificent), ankle socks: little picture. But
scrubbed twice a week in a fury by her grandmother, as though Siobhan were the stair, or
the tiles.

  The school, sitting in gravel and a bit of lawn,
facing the firth: always getting smaller in the

wind. Three rooms, two chimneys, corbie steps
but no corbie to climb them.

A school invaded by water and wind reaches
outside. There is little money so walks are
taken, pieces of the world are broken off and
taken back inside.

Write a report on a bird's nest. It must be
three pages long. It must be neat. It must be a
Scottish bird.

And dutifully she does so. Begins to write in
a small neat hand: nothing else will do but
smallness and neatness, so too in the white
house on the hill.

In spite of stricture she begins to love the nest
preserved in the school-room corner. Its speck-
led eggs. She begins to love it beyond all
bounds: her love grows wild, beyond the
hedgerow of penmanship.

She hears cut flowers blow in the wind of
where they were found; she begins to love the
rocks, the shells also sitting there, catalogued,
taken from inhospitable Scotland into the
desert of the classroom. The eggs die: nature
may function in the rain and wind but not under
the sharp eye of the dominie.

They learned their history in this way. Not
visors and pikes in worn books, but blown
through them by the wind, its odours, the rocks
and gorse all contain and give it, with a cry to
come together to a people betrayed by belief
and tantalized in the middle of their own
country.

In this way Siobhan begins to love things that
are old. There are enough in the white house,
generations of plainness, of knickknackery —
little porcelain treats.

She smells in the wind the sails of vanished
mills and barley dust from their stones. She
tastes in the water wrack which once lay in
blood on the beaches of Seaforth. She sees, in
the ashlar of the school wall, epitaphs.

And she still sees that dancing just stopped,
in that colour of stone. Anywhere, all her life.

She keeps these loves secret, for they are not
popular loves. Not a love of the clock or of the
calendar. It is not a love of *getting on,* with the
head down. Her love lets her see, and smile,
alone: in the dark. Clouds sweep like the hours
across the face of Scotland: it is too deep, it is
an art she has, not a love.

She spent a lot of time being dutiful; folding her
clothes, her grandfather's shirts. Just sitting,
the duty of looking at rain, the duty of heavy
food.

She spent hours in the tow of her grandmother, in kitchens: country women of different ages but all growing old, growing together
at the same rate, like a grove of laburnum,
whose flowers droop as the weight of petticoat,
skirt, pinnie and apron on Highland hips.

In kitchens, the lighthouse paraffin lanterns,

the coal fires glinted on shiny black pinafores, highly polished tiles, dark eyes creased with the amusement of gossip. Though gossip of an oddly moral character. What a strange community which even in the cocoons of kitchens cannot bring some things to be said.

Crockery jars, stags' heads in cool halls leading away from the kitchens. Dead things hanging. The pinnies the pantries the afternoon dainties – all were listening, disapproving judges. Some of these gatherings were in the kitchens of great houses, where her grandmother's friends worked; others in their own, but always the same greets and glimmers.

An idea glowered in these lights: an idea that women are and hold the true power of the world – an idea always lurking on the kitchen-stair of the Celtic mind. But the men of Scotland forged a weapon with which to best this power they feared: silence. In Scotland silence is lord, superior to the most heart-felt rage, however eloquent. To meet the most craven injustice with silence is to win.

Women in kitchens drinking tea, listening to silence surrounding them. In the face of the silence of men what is there to do but maintain? Wash the window, the steps, the clothing, the fireplace. Scrub down to the white bone of the world and see if silence reigns there!

Silence will look mean to God if it is scoured.

Here in the kitchen groves the laburnum women become ghosts, flitting in and out of their lot in life. Here sat Siobhan, a good little girl, skirt starched, socks white, little bag – children take the strangest things intae their heids don't they? O yes I ken – her hands washed. But love raged inside her for the things she saw around her: pinnies, stags' heads, jars, winds. A love she could not express without sweeping away everyone before her, all their fear and gossip and bauchles.

Siobhan grew a passion for her land, a passion equal to it: Scotland's best gift to her people. Truly her only gift.

Roll and tumble of tartan bedding. Is it you, mumbles McX, who likes my eyes in the morning? Thinks they shine, fawn-like?

He must be asleep! In pyjama bottoms he drifts into the Howff, a bar to be inspected. He floats among giant bottles and quiet conversation, sunlight falling through large half-frosted windows. The fruit machine chunks sullenly, under attack.

All in order. McX floats up near the ceiling, talk of football rising with the fag reek to buoy him. It's pleasant up here. The street door opens and a seal enters, wearing an anorak. The barman sternly puts his hands on the bar.

Now – Sir?

I am a man upon the land, I am a silkie in the sea –

What is it ye want?

Pint of special!

No. Oot. We don't need you silkies in here
with all yer doom and predictions and child-
snatching. Away oot. Nae trouble now.

All right for you, Jimmy! snarls the silkie. He
waddles out into the sunlight. Up in the sky
someone is playing a clarsach. The touch of
Siobhan: McX comes half awake. They make
love. McX hears the clarsach: Siobhan is without child. She breathes softly and returns to
sleep.

Far out in her Highland parish, every body was
in some state of decomposition. The quick and
the dead. In the rain and the granite living flesh
was grey, and hardly warmer than death.

The particular look of a small stone house
which has a corpse in it: something invisible
shuts over its dark clean windows. Something
stops dancing.

Siobhan was taken in to kiss the old woman
lying for a week in that time-refrigerated place,
for luck. The silence in that room, from the
other room. Siobhan was led in, she wasn't
afraid. There she was, lying in bed as she did
for months before she died. So: kiss: with the
naturalness of childhood and the naturalness of
death.

Only the adults mulled it over, roasting

themselves by the fire in the next room, stomachs tight, counting their aches and pains, ruminating. They're no very well. Outside, the bright hill, column of smoke, dark moving cloud.

Red and stupid eyes of the puff-faced undertakers from Inverness. Their humped hearse, polished, imposing, like a bourgeois Edinburgh villa on wheels, lacking only a little hexagonal stone chimney smoking on top. They looked overcome with grief, bags under their eyes from staying up all night with the body, gnashing their teeth and wailing – their black clothes dirty from throwing themselves down at gravesides, tearing up the sod. Their voices hoarse from making a high noise. They look as though they have been crying their eyes out. But between them they have shared most of the whisky and sandwiches.

Siobhan wakes and looks at McX, whose shoulders heave, longing for their quotidian covering of corduroy. She wants him.

Awake!

But he is profoundly asleep, out of his element in the castle bed.

Of the precision of Siobhan's desire: this love of things which was, unknown to her, an art, might have been seen in her, might it not?

And was seen, first in her handwriting. Then

in her tentative careful movement, which in years became grace. In her hands, in phantom colours in her eyes which were colours of things in the world she loved. Seen by her teacher, her first lover.

Siobhan was practised in secret love. So this furtive year of lit cigarettes waved in signal behind windscreens, baffling telephone calls, skirts raised up trying to resist the repleteness of lipstick, did not strike her as so unusual.

The surprise of finding warmth in another body in this huge grey landscape is the strangeness of Scottish love-making.

Her grandmother keeked inquisitively at her once or twice; grandfather suspected nothing. She was still a good girl. O especially when arched over a pillow, her hair entwined with her lover's.

It would never have occurred to her to make love in the white house, which sat and smoked and stared as before. That would have been obscene. If her grandmother and grandfather knew nothing, it was harder to conceal her flush from the green tiles, from the pinafore on its nail, from the army of jars in the kitchens she still visited. From the stags' heads, the owls in the great trees of the estates.

These only would issue the judgements she feared, for they, not her grandparents, were her guardians.

She had, and used, from her childhood a surprising hardness, to protect her loves. She would have felt little shame at the discovery of her love-making by the wifies, the dominies, the other children. But for the streams, the moving clouds of Moray to find out, or for those ? dancers in the graveyard to see, would have undone her.

For these reasons she never made love out of doors, no matter if she often wanted her lover very much if they walked, hands with lacquered nails joined, on the edge of the village or through the laburnum grove.

Strange to think that in those days a hundred miles across the Grampians a younger though not much else different McPint was already furiously pedalling the circus-bicycle of the schoolgirl obsession. Why? He hated school and it hated him. McPint imagined teachers had access to all the young flesh of Christendom. He could picture it thanks to pornography: necktie spanking. Badge sucking. McPint could never imagine one person drawn to caress another by penmanship, or eyes, or a way of touching the calendar. He could only think of thighs, flash-bulb mascara, knickers.

So did love exist, tossed like everything else in the dropleted winds of Moray. And into Siobhan with this love on the wind also came resignation. She did not get this requisite of life in her land the way others did, watching their fathers grind their teeth on their toolboxes or watching their mothers watch their fathers do this. Resignation came to her like mist, in bed,

on the tongue and in the eyes of her lover:
things are not like this, never were, will not be.

Resignation clicked, columnar, double-entry
over her eyes like a visor, when she was not on
the hills or in the great-house kitchens or in bed
with her lover. A visor alone is not protection –
but using it she saw her way through classwork,
examinations, folding her grandfather's shirts,
straightening her prefect's uniform (with which
she kept the others away, apart). The hardness
of eye-liner, the columnar regimentation of
stilettos.

The time came to leave. Without seeing the
art she had in her, she said she wanted to *learn*
some art or other.

The simple speaking of the word art brought
a terrible storm across the face and toolbox of
her grandfather, all his ancestors, all their
buried toolboxes. Deafeningly he set his jaw
and marched around the house in circles, days
on end. No more was said. Her grandmother
wept, soaking all the lavender handkerchiefs of
the region.

They bent Siobhan, they broke her. Or rather,
they changed her visor. They made for her a
new armour of nurse, of teacher. They put her
fine pale skin and her Highland eyes that
missed nothing and her beautiful brain into a
suit of armour out of the tired school-books.
Life is a battle, life is a fight to the finish with
the lords, the banks, with England, with the
Scottish departments! And pushed her off the

cliff of small minds into the pre-professional sea.

Something to do until you marry!

McX wakes and sees Siobhan's eyes glister. She is thinking of that cruelty of ago. In her eyes he sees those colours her first lover saw. McX moves toward her – with all her ghosts and love and remembering she smells of the Moray wind. It fires him, he takes her in his arms, takes her and all the boulders, cairns, lochs, brochs, rainwater. *Gathers* her and Scotland to him.

His beard on her lips, her breasts, that place her lovely teacher used to leave stained.

Outside the tartan room, down the stairs, the ancestors' wall-eyes persist.

McX's dromedary shape gives him ease of embrace: he is naturally curved for the im-partation of whispered endearments.

That is good.

More . . .

Just let me –

Now!

My country.

The politic of their love-making: he desires her, all her history. McX makes love to the tartan rug, the coal fire, to Beinn-a-Ghloe outside. Siobhan makes use of the moment's biology. She has been dreaming of her old lover and of Moray. Here is McX: surely he carries a seed of some sort. This is what she will have if she can.

A violence of fighting: thrusts of helmets from old books.

But in the end McX must relinquish. He must come away from love-making, as all men must, empty-handed, small-helmed. Women may come away with someone else.

Siobhan is happy: McX has lifted and carried her over the past pleasures of the Moray hills. He has won that little battle of the male against everything. But his tiny beetling army has not reached her; in Edinburgh the castle sits, still, shut on its rock.

McX looks at the ceiling in the dim firelight. Siobhan will not, cannot sleep in his arms. Along the roof-beams shuffle moody bears of paint.

Is this the one you will lie near from now on?

Siobhan looks at the depressed crescent of McX under the bed-clothes. A high tiny sound when he breathes out.

Is this the one?

Are you with me or are you no?

I am here.

That is not the same thing.

Contact, commitment, concupiscence difficult. For the men are hard ones, oh aye. But harder than the hardness of a little black dress? and pearls? and eye-liner? Cocktails calculated to make her interesting and an imaginary man interested? Hard, harder?

How explain the heady romance of dourness?

While McX drifts partly clad through history, mountains, saloon bars, Siobhan floats along a wet twisted dirty alleyway, behind the office of the Registrar. Convenient near the back-door of the undertaker, its frosted glass. She slips into the quiet lounge of a hotel of gentility. An immaculate carpet of slumber-making boke green: longcase clock.

Little black dress, she thinks, little black dress. To pay them back. To get some kind of power, but which this beautiful and powerful Highland woman already has, doesnae need. But her dreams of a little black power: to wear a classic little dress, beyond, subverting the safeness of her armour. Cross her legs in just the way and seduce some salesman silly-suit for no reason at all. Watch him play out his company-car performing dog act. *Hello* there.

Seduction learned and stored away when sophistication was an imported graphic, record covers seen at Rabbie's. In modern rooms drape-women smiled at men over dully grinning pianos, pillows of purple and gold, little black pianos, blond wood, paintings by the tomb-robbers of Kandinsky. *Seduction in Stereo.* Squelch of satin on brocade sofa: twilight cityscape, old-fashioned embrace reflected in aluminium cocktail shaker.

But why does she dream this way? Is this how we are to learn adulthood? Commercially, in a bag? Is this how to dream of power, of revenge? Dreams of seeing your lovers and other enemies bitterly panting, naked, beating the bodhrán?

Siobhan has her loves and her old love of loves. She observes the country of men and women through her softest and most secret socialist eyes: women sell themselves, on the street, in love, at the altar, in the kitchen. On record covers and in little black dresses.

Having kept herself apart from this, in her secret loves, she dreams to come outside herself, to revile what others made her do, dreams of a little black dress. To pay them back.

When Siobhan makes love with McX, she places her hand between them, turns her head away. Or there is a breath there, although he may not see. She will not wholly be with him because that is to give away all her loves, that is to sell. The little black dream dress keeps her out of the world. She need not take from any man the things they offer, freely and selfishly, dripping with that iridescent glue.

They wake and Siobhan tells this, that everyone is for sale. McX breathes with difficulty.

I must get back to my pipe!

Her argument shocks him, he feels ill. The beauty of her simplicity fills him with love, but he is sad, up against the ugly barrier of her words. Because she will not be sold, he can never have her, and yet that is why he truly loves her.

McX is mortified. But isn't he a silly man? Do you think McPint the monster would be surprised by Siobhan's argument? Do you think Totemic Smith the painter would find it wrong? Siobhan does float through her dream of seduction as a figurine in a Totemic Smith.

Siobhan and McX make love again and still she is without a child.

The world is roughly slept in and violently painted.

THE SPINDLES

McX sleeps and climbs high above Urgha on the Tarbert road. He drags on his cigarette and squints, looks out at the segmented world of the South Minch. Parts of this world blind him with sunshine. Others are invisible, hidden by the shadows of clouds and in banks of mist.

A small boat moves past toward sunlit little Scotasay, sections of its wake grey on black and elsewhere shining. Farther out, the waters of the sound also play this threatening, contrasting game. Black oceans move powerfully against small silver pools.

It will rain soon but he does not wish to leave.

He finds some grass free of sheep leavings and sits, glancing back at Urgha, where two columns of peat smoke stray in the wind of the approaching storm.

A dream the night before has enriched the magic he feels surrounding Siobhan. He wants to recall it. The first of the rain brushes his face.

Wooden spindles were known to come to the island through the air. Each spindle, softly touching down in the trees near Aird an Troim, bears the name of an islander and that of someone who will shortly enter his life. You do not need to walk in the wood and find your spindle – awakening on a morning you know it has come. You begin to wait for the one the spindle presages. Two spindles arrive for McX, one announcing Siobhan, the other, Aonghas.

Aonghas comes first, walking along the road on a light Saturday evening, carrying a cloth bag and his fiddle. He gets a job driving a tractor in Tarbert and plays his fiddle in the hotel at night. Aonghas drinks a great deal of the whisky. To put him in touch with his engorged musical heart.

McX is afraid when Aonghas plays at his most eloquent, pouring Gaelic from his violin, afraid the islanders will know Aonghas has come with a spindle. But Aonghas jokes and drinks and fights with them. They do not suspect.

Hill-walking one day, McX meets Siobhan by a peat stream. He knows who she is and asks her to walk with him. They share a love for the waters of sunset, for the way a white house sits on a hill. He asks her to lie near him, to share the sound at sunrise, asks that they marry.

Siobhan works at a nearly deserted farm. No one ever sees her in the village.

The music Aonghas plays illustrates McX's life with Siobhan. When they walk together among stones and peat banks, beneath the slow granite domes, McX hears Aonghas playing. Less often he catches sight of him beneath the brow of a hill.

Though no one is invited, McX hears Aonghas playing a glad air when he marries Siobhan at the manse. He wonders if she hears it.

Later, when McX puts their daughter to bed, he rocks her in his arms to the *balloo, ballaa* he hears outside. When McX calls to Siobhan, she keeps time with the reel he hears as she hurries to him.

Although one islander never speaks to another about the spindles, all know that those they herald will leave, long before the deaths of those they come to be with.

One evening McX waits for Aonghas at the hotel, but Aonghas does not come. McX shuts his eyes and hums the oldest tune he knows from Aonghas, but when he finishes he is still alone. His chest tight, he listens for music but cannot hear any. He sits, staring, afraid, for hours. Sits alone, listening for Aonghas all the night.

Morning, and McX runs from the hotel, out of

the village, hating knowing where he should go.

The sky is violent. He runs on, finally reaching a flat bank below Aird an Troim. Only now does he hear Aonghas, playing a lament so black and rich it freezes McX's heart.

He turns to see Siobhan as he first saw her. Now there are tears in her green eyes. McX reaches for her. She becomes pale, begins to fade away.

McX cries out. He hears some men calling to him. They point to the wood, tell him to look, but he turns away. He knows Siobhan's spindle is rising in the air and is flying toward a battlemented cloud.

McX falls down and the wind howls. He weeps in his dream, as fiercely as the rain pelts him now on the hill above the Minch. He jumps up and runs towards Urgha, toward the cottage he shares with Siobhan:

: down the stairs. Lands at the end of the long antler-hall. Room ⑰. Natural History Museum. Here the Visitor will find displays and Dioramas of Wildlife on the Estate. To one side of the large Collection of the Eighth Duke's fishing Flies will be found a very Odd monstrous Rabbit shot near the Burn in 1911.

Finds, in spite of and amidst this jungle of dusty breeks, fishing rods and more stuffed cervidae, something lurking of the strength and beauty of the land outside, through which he daily floats, compass-less, on a raft of ignorance and cigarettes.

Ah, wheezes McX, I must get back to my fishing.

Outside it is the same minute of morning it was when he entered; he floats three feet above the ground in his pyjamas.

Behind the castle the ground rises, until the burn runs in a narrow gorge. Here arches a stone bridge, obscured by trees. McX drifts over it, smoking cigarettes from a cornucopic dream pocket, toward the ruins of the old village. He sails over the ghillies' cottages, neat and severe in the morning fog and offering no proof the occupants are awake or even alive. The porticoes of rough-hewn tree trunks are painted forest green, decorated with antlers: the knify flurry that ends everything in Scotland – tangles of gorse, the endings of words, the mordents in pibroch. All these little ornaments pricks on the ends of quills. The extra roll of the R, the lilt of the redhead's tress-end.

McX floats in the mist, thrilled with love for it. He flies now back by the castle, glimpsing the little Highland room: Siobhan is in bed by the fire. McX picks up speed, his hair spills out behind him. He rockets down the avenue of trees, speeding toward the road and the station. The hotel appears before him, rushing up – he crashes helplessly though the roof and lands in his tossy bed, soiled with sweat and a wee boke he had in the night. And cigarette ash, and awakes.

Awakes? caked with nicotine sweat, sleep-sand, and spittle dried in his beard as if a snail has crossed him. Perhaps one has – the window is open and the morning is dewy.

III

FEUDAL GESTURES

A lake without a fisherman, streams without a miller, pastures without a shepherd, road without a wayfarer . . . Disquiet without cause.

Karel Čapek, A Journey to Scotland

But the reality of it was as reality often is: sad, and different.

Begin with what the eye can see: house and tree and field. November, wrestling with mildness. A small group of old stone outbuildings and a byre. A ewe has wandered behind the rusted iron yett and now, like a fly of autumn, cannot figure how to get out. But unlike a fly she only stands and stares, instead of hurling her all at that which cannot give.

The relations between these things may be a useful map of the estate.

The two small chimneys of a stone cottage smoke in the wind. On the doorstep is a large sea shell, at the back door a woodpile. The cigarette of McX slowly smokes inside the cottage. Here, waking, he now lives with Siobhan. The pink inside of the sea shell seems still alive. Filled with dew in the morning sun it may be. Late the home of some middling gastropod, how appropriate that it sits on McX's sill. McX lives in this house like a nautilus. He moves slowly through its rooms, never wanting to go back into one once left. He is observed with amusement by Siobhan. He professes his love for her; she accepts his caresses, strokes his shoulders which stoop horizontally in bed.

McX struggles with the woodpile. In sun coming low across the fields, making the stone walls of the cottage glow, he applies himself with cigarette and dull hatchet to diminishing the tangle of branches, sticks, purloined planks and crate-ends Siobhan is always storing up. Here is the cottage, here the sea shell, here enough wood being hacked up by McX to build another house. Think of the homeless.

The woodpile fills the spiritual horizon of McX. It swells with humidity, frustration, the forlorn and infinite sense of duty.

McX and Siobhan attend their fire like an eternal lamp. McX thinks of this as their love; Siobhan puts no name to it.

They pay more attention to the fire than to each other. If they should go to town at night, and return to find the fire out, they are desolate. They quarrel. They go to their cold bed and do not make love if there is no fire.

Siobhan has made the fireplace an altar. She has developed a rite, a mass for it. Scrubbing it, wiping it, brushing it. She approaches, slowly, bits of firelighter in her hand like wafer, the ash-pail swings in her other hand, a censer. The mantel white as snow, crowned with two candlesticks of laburnum wood, and the monstrance of her grannie's ancient biscuit tin.

The renting of the cottage from my lord's factor

was on this wise.

Aye, we have a few properties available, Sir – strictly on a rental basis to parties of a circumspect character.

McX tried to straighten his back, thinking the soul might live there the day.

What is it you do, if I may ask?

Weights and Measures.

You're a gauger.

Aye.

God damn you to hell if I may say so. I mean, considering his lordship's business and that.

Hm!

Why do you wish to live out here?

McX thought of his house, of the soiled draught-excluders, the cigarette-browned reading lamp, the derelict kitchen, frightening midnight visits of McPint. The horrible name of Allotment Street flashed through him.

I find the town too busy.

Are you a married man?

No.

But – ?

I have an . . . attachment.

I see. [Scottish Official Breath.] His lordship doesnae believe in housekeeping without benefit of clergy. But. Ehhh. Seeing you are an officer of the Crown. I could – ehh – let you have the west gate-house for fifty pound per calendar month.

May I see it?

I'll give you the key. It's much too damp and

horrible for me to enter. My chest.

And so McX stood in a dark little house, the leavings of bats birds and mischievous boys all at his feet. Smoking, he looked out at the fields. Cattle, crows, sheep, and many stones. A man, shivering violently in a plastic windcheater, tugging at one. His job of the day. Och.

A tiny cottage, a dirty mouldy cottage unused to people. Yet a house Siobhan would make home, and beautiful, basing its beauty on the comforts and subtleties of the view from this window. Stands of forested trees: within the largest grove, in the distance, what my lord calls his castle. Ha. My lady cannot even call it home.

The day on which McX proposed this arrangement to Siobhan, he went into town. His dromedary coat was brushed, his collar for once near symmetry. All in our town suffer from *collara:* a disorganizing fever which points the ends of cheap collars this way and that. He stood in the open door of the Auld Licht, a cold pint of lager in the one hand and a fresh gently smoking cigarette in the other. He squinted: his mannerism.

At six-thirty he came out and began slowly to wander up the street, pausing at the organ-shop window, the Campbells are coming ta ra ta ra. He glanced too at the upper shelf in Smillie's.

But McX is not one for the magazines of men, their stink and thumb-essences of McPint.

By systematically dawdling ta ra ta ra he gradually arrived in front of the only open door on the street, that of the Bengal Tandoor Mahal, where Siobhan, wearing a neat tweed jacket and a flowered skirt, was waiting.

Balajiprasad was happy to see them. He was happy to see anyone on a weekday night. Because it was Siobhan, who like every woman in town he had propositioned, Balajiprasad made the great flourishes of restaurateuring of which only he in this our town is capable, or culpable. In dramatically polishing the plates he smacked McX in the mouth with his towel. Siobhan laughed.

Of Siobhan's sense of humour: mostly predicated on the physical misfortunes of others. An unfortunate, though not a cruel sense of humour, though the butts of it cannot often be induced to see it so.

Siobhan watched McX squirm, first from Balajiprasad's drooling and fawning, then from the menu and the food, then from the inexplicably rising heat in the empty stale restaurant.

McX hunched, closer to the table. He was still in the dromedary, sweating like a devil, his hands shook as he so clumsily brought the conversation round to they two, trembled so even in the lighting of his cigarette of sophistication. The banal cigarette of constant need now turned into an object of art, and so held in a slightly different way, looked at more often, more carefully. It becomes a different thing, a mace of the authority of suavity instead of a breathing apparatus.

Siobhan thought of the other places in our little town where she might have been taken and asked this thing. Where she had been asked, before. A wine bar where a man in a late-registration pin-stripe suit had once courted her, and while she had liaisons and pretensions in her mind toward this group, she knew she was too strange for those men.

A bit too wild, a bit too beautiful, too rainy, musical, and much too Scottish. These men with the bulging eyes and an English idea of elegance and an American idea of sameness couldn't face her, their own country. So the wages of individuality is McX in an Indian restaurant.

Too, there was the hotel, where in her floating dream of little black dresses there were men to offer love or at least marriage, but the reality of the hotel was *very* different and *very* sad. It was dank and idiotic, and Siobhan knew McX had nothing but contempt for their optics and the slimy pistons of their beer engines, their mock Georgian furniture and clean carpet.

Siobhan's heart was moved toward this pretty wretched man, to this bloke with the inescapably Scottish job and existence and cigarette and dromedary coat.

Not *be mine,* as in books or the pictures. Not *will ye hae us,* as in the indigenous. Just: *let's.* Siobhan thought of her winter coat hanging singular on the hook at home. Thought of how she had traded the hills and birds of her love and mind for wet grey houses suffering under yellow vapour lamps, thought of the smell of the chippie and everyone's damn fags. McX, elbow crooked in sophisticated mid-drag squint, slowly leaned in mint sauce. Pity and amusement warmed her.

All right then.

McX was something to protect and enjoy protecting. Purity of enjoyment didn't trouble Siobhan. For her that was for hills, and a lover's hand of ago. McX wouldnae be so bad looking, without the depressed look he had, waiting for her answer. If only he could somehow trim his beard to gentler effect. And he, or someone, could press his trousers a wee bitty more often than once in a while.

For Siobhan it might be a return to the whole mind, to the whole of a landscape she had been, and left. And she might love him for that. There were things she would hold back from him, oh aye, you lose the capability of abandon, don't you? It's of debatable value to find yourself abandoned in this weather.

McX has nowhere to store the rusty items one

can never banish. A shed, by mail, of wood, is
the thing. Aye. So, orders it. By mail a shed! For
several weeks McX paces up and down the
corner of the midden where it is to stand. He
smokes in contemplation of this noble rectangle, delicately fingers the blades and tines of
all his junk currently leant crazily in the little
back hall.

Arrival of collapsed shed. Uncomfortable
assembly of it by McX. Siobhan watches with
amusement: his fingers cold and dry in the
November air, tweaked by the rough edges of
badly-machined flanges and nuts.

The pathos of watching a man working hard
at something in the wrong clothes, stiffly bending, the wrong shoes, bad little tools that fit
nothing, and all the while trying to smoke. One
twist of the spanner and the smoke drifts up
into his eyes and he must stop to paw them.

McX stands with his legs prideful, apart, in
the shed now complete. He brings a chair in
and briefly considers it as living space. The
smell of new boards exerts its age-old hypno-
tism on the male.

From the kitchen Siobhan sees him as she
used to see her grandfather retreat into his
greenhouse, and pauses at her washing, slightly
sad.

But now the shed stands, bursting with tools
and spools of wire of which McX is ignorant but
shamefully proud. Another little link with tech-
nology, system, masculinity.

But how strongly is it bolted together? McX has only the weak arms of the cigarette smoker.

A week later, a strange noise at the front door. McX has been dreaming under the reading lamp and shuffles there in dromedary dressing-gown. Upon the doorstep is my lord, what a fright to see.

In the early winter sun his lordship is an ancient pink and flushed individual, his nostrils wet and dilated, horse's nostrils. Behind him steams his car, as though a madman has parked. It is a surprise to see his lordship outside of it. Proof he can walk still. It is a surprise to McX to see snorting things like these in his front garden. His lordship snorts and breathes in rhythm with the indignance of his machine.

Is that shed of your erection? asks his lordship.

Aye, says McX, breathing out a lot of smoke on my lord.

Do you not know that all erections must be cleared with the factor?

McX's eyelids flutter briefly as he thinks what McPint would say to this. *Losh, I'd be up there twenty times a day, man! I'd need a building permit eh!*

My factor that is, says his lordship.

What's the matter with it? says McX. He squints.

I find it grossly – ramshackle.

Another drag on the cigarette. Do you want

me to tear it down?

Assiduously.

Ye'll owe me a hundred pound.

Ha!

What about ma things? says McX. They'll rust.

A fig for rust, offers his lordship.

But now the mediaeval light dies from my lord's face. His lordship's legs are spindly, uriny, shaky inside their tailored twin tweed towers. My lord is tired of the world of men, men who do not obey him as they used, or ought. When he was but newly a peer and the whole of his bride was able to distract him from the holes in the walls of his stupid castle. His lordship gave her pleasure in those days.

McX sees this, some old solar system sweeping across my lord's dusty-rose face of resentment. It is remarkable that a man of his lordship's stature in the business of getting folk drunk, owner of the lion's share of this huge county, should have nothing better to do than stand on McX's unswept broken slab of a sill and piss himself over a shed. His lordship narrows his eyes and fumbles in his stalking jacket for a wee cahier of the finest doeskin.

Are you the gauger? asks his lordship.

Aye, says McX.

God damn you to hell is what I say!

And stalks off, away back to the loyal huffing motor car. His lordship makes a great show of gear selecting, backing and revving. Points out the window at the shed as he drives off:

You must *register . . . notify . . . apply . . . !*

My lord's red face barking verbs of requirement and statute disappears down the track toward the big stand of trees. Flutter of ghillie caps coming off in the fields.

My lord is not of a noble family. He was created a peer for his services to industry. That is, he kept the Yanks drunk as skunks when they were fools enough to pass a national law against it. The thirst of regret was deep.

Of course theirs turned out to be only a prohibition of decency, but his lordship and his like never complained. They knew all would come right in the end. The problem was to keep the profits up until it did. Never say his lordship never brought pleasure to anyone.

Even in those days, when his lordship had the first private motor car in the county, and electricity glowed from single light bulbs in a handful of farm houses, his lordship was able to buy half of this shire. From some truly noble old bastard who'd been had by the death duty and done by drink. My lord's drink if truth be told.

A castle there was. Oh aye. From Pictish times, always something there. And his lordship for many years tried to live in it. Fifteen years ago he pulled it down in a rage and built a modest pebble-dash bungalow. The wind used to come into the castle, and wake him, and get at him, and wake my lady and make her complain – it eventually made her ill and what is worse indifferent to my lord's touch. A wind that blew across his lordship from the past, at least as he imagined it, a wind which roughened his skin and made his eyes red and flattened back his ears into a rat-like determination that all the little Scots men and women of the twentieth century around him were still peasants. OCH. AYE.

He didn't bother asking anyone: simply looked about him in the Lords one day and decided they were all a clutch of snoozy twits, all doing things a deal worse than pulling down their ancient inherited uncomfortable piles. They all had piles from the look of 'em.

And this bungalow is now the castle. Wintersgill's wife, who serves my lady, must speak of working 'inside the castle walls'. Even though it's a' double-glazin and a semi-hollow Georgian front door just like Cambeul the butcher in the town.

God bless Thatcher, house of Thatcher for our new heritage of ersatz Georgian doors.

Her ladyship has secreted a garden gnome, as a jest. Although she didn't like the old castle either.

His lordship leases out much of his land to farmers, and some of the old cottages as to McX and Siobhan, and drives about, worrying about sheds. His lordship is worn by care beyond reason or understanding.

When he was at the height of his industrial
nobility, his lordship built the fashionable thing.
In centuries past this would have been a wee
castello d'acqua or follied park; but in 1930 it
was the *model village* – the caring face of
feudalism.

Two rows of stone cottages that were clean
instead of dirty, plumb instead of squint. For a
time. And a church which was very empty, and
a store no one ever took on. And my lord named
the village after himself.

His lordship farmed then and a few folk lived
there for a while. But as there was nae shop and
nae school, and as it wasn't near anything at all,
being built at the bottom of a bog, they all
eventually buggered off.

Sometimes his lordship will drive dov'n to the
empty and overgrown model village, when he
has profound need of irritation. Wintersgill is
sometimes employed unsticking the few working drains there.

Wintersgill removes his cap which sticks on
his abundant eyebrows. Cold air blasts his
unhaired head.

Morning my lord.

Ah. It's –

Wintersgill, my lord.

Yes. Wintersgill.

He knows damn well who it is! A little snow
brushes his lordship and Wintersgill down in
Model-Village-in-the-Bog. An open pipe or
broken window gives up a low whistle. A

rattling of old locks, the keys gone from the face of the earth. His lordship says nothing and Wintersgill goes back to tugging at a suspiciously knotted root system.

Bit of life in the old place yet, Wintersgill.

My lord.

Tell me – did you ever live here, man?

Och no, my lord, I was born at the west yett. But ma faither lived here when it were new.

Does he speak well of it?

He doesnae speak o' naething, my lord – he's deid of consumption thirty year.

Of course it is not possible the man Wintersgill could say the right thing to my lord. Indeed no one can. But the purple face thundering suddenly away leaves little doubt in Wintersgill he has said something offensive.

It's the sack for me, Wintersgill says aloud.

Wintersgill never had the idea of joining a union and he doesnae even ken who he actually works for. His lordship is there, that's all Wintersgill kens.

His lordship is not satisfied: the land must be made to pay. It must yield up its rodents and birds.

Italians come. His lordship gets them fou. Steamin fou. They like to laugh and get steamin fou in the castle. They get so fou these Italians that they forget what a curious castle it is. Not

like your castles in Italy no. But that's the
English for you.

Scottish, growls his lordship from the gun-
room.

O, scusi, *Scozzi,* scusi. Ha ha ha!

In the fields and woods, the Italians march,
shooting. Anything which moveth. They're
moving. They shoot themselves. They are so
fou on his lordship's whisky and so happy to
have paid a thousand pound a day and so elated
to be picking the shot out of their thick legs and
bulging bottoms. Never say my lord never
brought pleasure to anyone.

During Italian season life is dangerous on the
estate. Wintersgill is regularly sprayed with
lead and McX quickly learns to keep down and
run for the bus. He considers painting c o w on
his coat as farmers did in war. It is war, and all
the men and women of his lordship's estate lost
long ago.

It took McX a time to get the lay of the local
tradesmen. In the office, MacKenzie sidled up
to him.

You're living out on the estate now?

Aye.

The coalman out there is nae good. Always
gives short weight. You'd better keep your eye
on him.

Measuring whisky is MacKenzie's religion;

the gauging of coal is his hobby. But while McX
had become indifferent to the wrath of cheating
barmen, he feared the deliverers of coal. They
were enormous. So Scottish God was presented
with the sight of one of his own men of weight
and measure cowering under the bed when the
brutish coalmen came.

Did you get fair weight? asked MacKenzie.

Oh aye, said McX, nae problem at all.

But in the shed it looked a poor ten hundred-
weight. Siobhan looked McX up and down in a
way that filled him with dread.

The cottage into which Siobhan brings arte-
facts of the world and arranges them, pleasing-
ly, with smooth cool touches, is as damp as the
factor said. McX keeps little paraffin burners
alight, to take the chill off the chill. The paraffin
is brought up the long estate road by a smiling
man.

McX, taking advantage of the new-found
freedom of the countryman, is pissing out his
front door one morning. The kye gather, as they
will for anything, to watch. Out the corner of his
eye McX sees the smiling paraffin man
approaching in his car. And knows that from
that distance all the man can see is McX waving
his pintle at a group of cows.

Fine day, says the paraffin man. Smiling.

McX is filled with lurid ideas – the stories the
smiling man will tell in the public house at
night. We have no reason to trust smiling
people in Scotland.

A few weeks later McX, in a state of exhaustion, tells this story to McPint, who frowns, actually thinking of Bambi.

All he saw was me wavin my thingmie, ye ken, burbles McX.

Aye, says McPint absently, I ken what ye mean. My wife's a cow and she willnae suck *me*.

The sun is known in Scotland, but chiefly through myth and legend. As the brighter comets are to the rest of men, the sun has been seen by Scots and it is probable it will return. But it falls back, sucking its thumb, a child at the parents' cocktail-hour; it never comes fully out to show off its yellow frock or do its little dance.

Here in this little land from which the tools of atom war might well first emerge, 'brighter than a thousand suns' means little. There isnae one to judge it by.

Appearance of chicken-flesh at the first jerk of the thermometer: Scots in the sun. What need to brown yourselves? You'll be roasting in Hell soon enough.

Roll and tumble of Scottish clouds. St Clement's Day, an inclement day for Clement, lashed to an anchor and pitched into the ocean for his trouble. After he cracked rocks and brought forth water and all the rest of it. He possibly made a lamb appear. Think of the

ticket mannie, spilling his pipe from the poop
deck – ! But the angels built Clement a beautiful
home under the waves.

Wintersgill in the field, in a plastic garment
promotional of tools, pulls at a stone. Gradual
assembly of crows on a wire fence. Pruk, pruk,
pruk. Wintersgill desists from pulling at the
stone. He has many months to remove it. The
tractorman pointed it out as a particularly ugly
piece of trouble when the fields were laid to rest
after harvest. Wintersgill is methodical, and
wrong: a few good tugs a day, he thinks, will
have it out in only a few weeks' time. He has no
idea how this stone is part of an immense
boulder, breathing, mean-minded under the
soil.

He stops dead in the middle of the hard field.
Pruk, pruk, pruk! His attention is drawn to the
crows. Pruk! Of a sudden they look familiar.
Wintersgill cannot read music but he can
recognize it: black blots arranged on five lines.

Superstitious Wintersgill sees that music has
been given him here in the cold, and he is
afraid. He thinks of his wife, ill in their cottage.
Music here, death there under the tight dome
of this day, which will freeze before the sun
finishes its plaintive balcony-scene.

His wife dying in their stale bed, misunder-
stood by grave wee Wintersgill, begrudged by
my lord and my lady. Indeed it makes little
sense that here in this negligible area, not glen
and not town, a wide and workmanlike scatter-

ing of only a few stone houses and tired easily-worked land, Scottish God should send down death. He must have spilled some; there is no reason for Wintersgill's house to be targeted, a black bullseye. God shouldnae punish the stolid. But there is a little death's head everywhere, for the renewal everyone speaks of. Well – Scottish God does have all the time in the world and Wintersgill does not. Not even time to remove the stone.

Here is music, written bold in your system by fence crows. Only a happenstance but proof that music comes and goes. All the time, inside rocks, in eddies, especially in the movements of trees. Suppose you stood with Wintersgill, you saw the crow music moment. Ceol dubh. Even though the day is cold you might conceive a wish to write this music down.

Dash for the bus, duck the hunters, arrive at the tomb of the stationers, request staff-paper, a pen:

Oh no, Sir – nothin like that!

Draw your own lines? Fegs! It's no proper music paper. You cannae do *onythin* right.

Correct pen and paper not available, Wintersgill's wife dyin in there, the crows about to fly.

Siobhan brings the hills, the air, the warmth she can find trapped even in rime into the cottage. McX goes about his job and sees McPint and the interior of the Auld Licht less than occasionally, bless God. Travelling up and down B roads and long saloon bars, McX can pause to think, ardent, of Siobhan, the fire, the colours awaiting him in their home.

So different a home than Allotment Street or that of his childhood. Textile, stone, the quiet decoration she has brought, her decorousness. McX feels for the first time awake in his own dwelling-place. He neglects his usual dream-spot under the reading lamp, the industrial nature of which is castigated by Siobhan.

Perhaps you know what it is like to be newly housed with one you love. It is said there is a peculiar, hunger-fulfilling quiet, a joy to be found in washing and repairing; and every evening the night seems long, full of possibility and invitation. Perhaps you can tell how happily people go to bed together.

After their supper there is a time by the fire. They speak quietly, drink a little whisky. McX changes in these hours, ceases to be an object of amusement and pity to Siobhan, perhaps even at all. Forgetting job, McPint, the wood-pile, smoking, the soul and shape of him straightens to the merest suggestion of dromedary. Siobhan cannot see his beard is not ship-shape, doesn't smell the fag reek. For a short time in these short times they love.

A small ritual emerges whereby, holding each other, they look into the mirror and essay ideas of play.

I like to see your hand grip the bed-linen.

May I tie a ribbon on you?

Soon they leave the fire after carefully banking it up.

Winter is stamping his feet and whistling in their house himself. McX luxuriates on an electric blanket, somewhat as he was used to do under the hot reading lamp of Allotment Street. In only his vest, his thighs and thingmie tingle with illicit wicked warmth. He revels and glories with attention that is marvellously far from dream. And Siobhan comes to him.

McX begins to seek this nightly stimulation, this brief electric randiness, as much as the fireside lips of Siobhan, her eyes, the whisky glasses and dried flowers in the flickering light, her words suggestive and loving in the mirror. But Siobhan, tired after many weeks of ardour, learns that to leave McX on the griddle of his winter bed just long enough will put him to sleep – dark, pink, mouth-wet. Then should she wish it Siobhan can linger by the fire, or stand outside, by the sea shell, with a secret cigarette under the moon. By herself. By herself.

Somewhere in Scotland a rat is gnawing. Scrunch, munch. Nibbling at the edges of the green table-lands where McX is dreaming. The coast near Aberdeen?

Blackwood is his dream when they are happy,

Hephzibah when they are not.

A daughter imagined, and kept to himself these years. Between the pages of his encyclopaedia. A beautiful child, now of his love for Siobhan. A dark and quiet child with large eyes, and dresses of Siobhan's inspiration – no smack of your High Street tartan smocks.

In the late afternoons of imagination, on street corners tending toward Scotland of the Night, McX and Blackwood make their way home. With what love, with what trust does she put her hand in his – how McX's heart grows when she does this.

McX, the civil-serving, chain-smoking dromedary, thinking himself unobserved, doing his messages in the High Street, has closed his large hand round a little one of air, and stepped across the road. He walks slowly but does not betray her in any other way.

Alone sometimes on the inch at noon, having smoked, having devoured his biscuits, McX might point out to her a flower or a duck, his voice low and full, not unlike the way he speaks to Siobhan in the mirror.

McX dreams of showing Blackwood all Scotland. In dream he has understood and loved it, as never he has when awake, seeing it through the smudged glass of an automobile. In the Scotland McX shows her, all is right if not pretty. She takes pleasure in the same things as he: the spaces between trees, the knowledgeable brain of mist, the ceol beag to be found at the bottoms of fences and hedge roots.

McX takes Blackwood room by room through his castle-giant dream of Scotland; she was born to Siobhan in the small bed in the turret.

Blackwood takes his hand and together they walk away from Scotland of the Night, from the vapour lamps, from McOcalypse, from the layers of smoke and the ¼ and ⅕ gills. In his dream of Blackwood McX is so happy he does not even smoke. His spirit grows huge, bursting out of his lungs.

If only Siobhan could love McX who dreams Blackwood.

From McX Blackwood learns sorts of love, what skills he has, and facts. Not the folk history of smoking and lager-brewing his browy head is stuffed with; thank Christ he leaves the football out. In McX's dreams Blackwood learns history, on which awake he hasn't the slipperiest hold, only a fine osmotic sense of betrayal. Blackwood grows to finer, more compassionate versions of McX's eye-crinkle, scepticism, bravery.

From Siobhan Blackwood learns music, music before this clumsier alphabet. Siobhan's movements become hers: her hands, her grace, her eyes full of the hills cloud and water around them. Fear and pity for the hard life things have. Silent reproachment for excess, in this child McX has made in dream with Siobhan. Show her the world is something to caress change into, and pleasure from – instead of a thing to be stamped on, screamed at and the gut torn out of: that will be a graceful Blackwood.

Teach her to see, and thinking on what she sees to compare it with all she knows: that will be a strong Blackwood. Not always pleased with others, who do not think but only take, but that will be a whole Blackwood.

Such is Blackwood when McX dreams her or when he stops to see her in the green touches in Siobhan's eyes, in the grace of her hands. Siobhan, who cannot guess what he is staring at.

Domesticity is a kind of slow torture not recognized by the authorities. Late afternoon: a ray of sun falls through the kitchen window of McX. He is standing, smoking, leaning against the sink. Ash falls on the draining board. Here may be a reason the sun is feared in Scotland: we are drawn to whatever the odd ray picks out. Will stand milling about, considering it, for hours. In McX's kitchen light falls on a recipe pinned to the green hopsacking of the notice-board. Here Siobhan keeps pieces of paper which add up to the household scheme. The slow eye and brain of McX are brought to a yellow clipping from one of the hare-brained magazines that keep the flowers of Scotland in thrall. *Crispy Pilchard Bake.*

Somethin nae good about *crispy*. It's futile: in

all our dampness we have no knowledge of, no
right to crispy. And pilchard! Agh. Something
wet and fusty about that. McX might have
grown up on Pilchard Street. Pilchard Street,
Dunfermline – there is truth here. And *bake*.
Bake, a noun! We're havin a bake for oor tea the
night. A boke more likely. *Bake* sloughs up dry,
in the back of McX's throat: a powdery horror
of a word, the back of McPint's throat, why he
produces such awful words and sounds.

Its casserole pots, its magazine recipes the
downfall of Scotland. Served up to the dinner
table every Scotland of the Night, an unlikely
enurnment of the nation's history. Try the potatoes this way and that. So many potatoes in the
world. Milk, cream, eggs, fish, milk, cream,
eggs, fish. Jammy piece bake. Och. No matter
how McX's spirits may fly with Siobhan's when
they make love, when they sleep, when he
dreams – when he eats he eats something
crusty in a pot. We all do. O where is the eating
of Scotland of old? The meat and the tatties that
made men sae bold? For Burns Night last year
we had to eat cold: a fish supper washed down
with Irn Bru.

McX dumps his cigarette in the sink and
reaches in the beam of sun for the recipe,
source of his indeterminate waist and the
historical complications of his digestion. Rips it
from the drawing-pin, crumples, destroys,
damns this devil's document to the bin.

Go to hell, says McX, I'm no eatin this.

Dumps it in the bin along with himself and the rest of us and our history. Whatever Crispy Pilchard Bake you're being fed, it's odds-on they know the recipe by heart.

THE BLACK DINNER

In matters of gaiety we in our county have only a grey newspaper for guide. After consulting its hideous advertisements with doubt, McX and Siobhan, to whom an evening's entertainment meant anything but this, arrived somewhat timorously at an indifferent country house now catering to the whims of the petty bourgeois.

McX's dead friend Kyehouse thought this place regal, imagine. But bad carpeting knows no boundary. Damn the cost: 'elegance' can't do anything about scuffed bottles of tonic water.

McX and Siobhan went there to celebrate. Celebrate what: that MacKenzie, that Wintersgill now knew they lived together in the cottage? That his lordship hadn't thrown them out? To prove they had a little money now and then?

How celebrate in the midst of farmers?

McX, uncomfortable as he had ever been, stiff as with cold, sat at a linen table, subdued and repressed by the feel of his collar. Siobhan was suffering perhaps its female equivalent, or was irritated by McX's collar. All round them the liberties and abandon of farmers.

To till the soil might be thought a straightfor-
ward life, if not a restful, for dependable honest
men. But there must be shame and dread in it,
for the farmers of our county are driven to
destroy themselves and all their kind. *Oblivion*
is what they seek from the earth. Are they
ashamed at poisoning the hills in order to
extract the ever more bounteous parsnip? No –
they do not think of such things. What they
think of: each other's wives.

Not to connect their schemes with some
hearty feeling of Brueghel.

Other wives and gallons of whisky is what
farmer Broon thought of at his table. He had
sized up Siobhan. He knew something about
her. He had watched her at the bus-stop from
his plush motor car. But her strangeness had
damped his chicken-house lusts: farmer Broon
always stopped thinking about anything he
didnae understand.

His idea of Siobhan was that she was uncan-
ny, and therefore cheap, available; but that she
would unsettle him. So his eyes roamed the
mail-order curves of the wives of Grudie, Allan,
and Stewart. Some merchants of the town who
made the same money as farmers and dressed
like them were there too: Smillie, Cambeul.

Farmers have their own aristocracy, but it is
not *the* aristocracy. My lord hates farmers, to
him they are ugly machines, no different from
ploughs and reapers.

We are all in check in this county. Our shire is like a chess set. The set, not the game. O there is wiliness here and there, some crude wee strategies, but you will have seen that mate is difficult. Chess set, model village, black and white, war divided and orderly. A set of feudal figurines: the queens in conical head-dresses get around a lot more than the men. The queens have the most power. They have felt bottoms. Oft. The kings are slow-moving cats of privilege like his lordship. The knights and bishops, merchants and tenant-farmers, Smillie, Stewart, hurrying to do what they are bid. Wintersgill and his blank kind the pawns – stalwart, eyeless, in doublets and carrying little seed-bags. And awaking one morning you might find one of the castles of our county had stolen surprisingly up to your house in the night. And then what would you do eh?

Broon was at home in the decor of this hotel. Though some of it mismatched, it was holy hoovered every day. Here was no stench of the village hall, cigarettes and slopped 80/-, the ticket mannie's Err-Na-More, where Broon went on Tuesday nights. Ostensibly to observe a snooker club, really to stare furtively at the daughters of tractormen.

Farmer Broon has a decent living. He has a number of side-lines, hay and free-range eggs. Free-range eggs are for zealots; the couthy will avoid them. What is healthy about an egg birthed by a chicken of Broon's yard, where

Jaguar-oil, complex chemicals and farmer Broon's own midnight vomit mingle? Chickens ought eat nice washed seed.

Broon was here without his wife. She thought he was at a meeting. If she knew he was dining here she wouldnae have believed it. He had never taken her anywhere. She was a prisoner of her pinny and her kitchen.

Following his agrarian libido, Broon was here to pursue his affair with The Widow. There are many widows among farmers as the men are forever shooting each other. Bored, fou, armed, stupid – why not? These murders are the chief recreation of our county, read about with glee from my lord to Wintersgill.

Broon had a problem: The Widow was late. How would he explain to his wife his unreturn at the hour the phony meeting was to end? He wanted to spend the night with The Widow, in one of the strangely plush rooms. Farmer Broon's eye roved the dining room, searching for help. It lighted again on Siobhan, and McX.

Why hadn't the wily Broon thought of him before? McX's was the only voice in the room his wife wouldnae know! Broon's wife like all farm wives knew and suspected the whines and plaints of the men. The attempts of Smillie at a foreign accent, the feigned drunkenness of Grudie. Always in the night these louts are telephoning with the improbable.

Broon took a sip of his dram and went over to McX's table. His farm redness and his wiry silver hair, his liquid eyes signalled to Siobhan what was up. She blushed. McX barely unfolded himself, out of laziness and also for fear his collar would rip his neck open, gushing out.

Evening, Mr McX.

Aye.

It's a fine evening the night.

I suppose so.

I wonder if might ask you a wee favour.

McX hadn't a clue what farmer Broon might want of him. Siobhan's eyes deepened, as they always did when she called the spirits and winds of Moray to judge someone.

If you'd excuse us, Mrs, I'll explain – , said Broon.

McX found himself leaving the table, leaving Siobhan and her eyes full of warning. Found himself fawningly manoeuvred to a telephone grotto by Broon.

It's the wife, don't you see – ? said Broon. She thinks I'm at a meetin.

He gave an ugly cackle.

What'm I supposed to do? said McX.

Broon turned red.

Well, I'm here with The Widow, y'see. Just say I've been called away to a committee meeting in Aberdeen, and cannae be home till tomorrow. They're puttin us up in a hotel.

Aberdeen! said McX.

Aye, said Broon, I'd be much obliged. Just this once.

McX felt alone at sea. The idea that this was a

part of country life broke upon him, something endemic to the bleak and scattered community. Rules are rules. What would Siobhan say?

I'll happily stand ye a malt for yer trouble, said Broon.

And Broon was big; in his ruddiness he could easily be imagined angry. McX took the ten pence and dialled the number Broon gave him.

Is this how men and women live thegither? McX began to doubt his cottage, their fire. Thinking out the detail of this big lie, he was frightened by the beauty, the loveliness of the answering voice –

Hullo, said McX.

Broon slipped away to the bar.

I'm callin for Mr Brood, said McX belatedly pinching his nose, that was what one did. I'm callin from the committee. We're havin tae go to Aberdeen, there's an emergency meetin there and they're puttin us up in an hotel.

Who is this?

Och, ye dinna ken me, my name's McPint, flushed McX.

Well, all right, Mr McPint, if that's what's necessary. I'll expect him home tomorrow then.

Right, cheero then, said McX.

Goodnight, Mr McPint!

McX put down the telephone. He turned to discover Broon with a large whisky in his hand, his face a concoction of childish delight and very tired adult dirtiness.

I thank you, said Broon theatrically.

McX took the whisky without speaking and went in to Siobhan. Her colour was high and her eyes spoke a lot of something in another language. The whisky tasted foul to McX, who sat, still waiting for his starter in this hell, grieving over the loveliness of Mrs Broon's voice, a voice he had no reason to wrong. Later he would be troubled in sleep by the sound of it; he ought to do the decent thing and marry her.

The Widow entered the room, the eyes of all the county's farms on her. She and Broon began to wallow in the temporary sty of their desire. Ugly and shallow Widow, triumphant over the beautiful voice of the telephone.

In the middle of his mud, Broon's eye wandered to McX, and some glint of it made McX certain Broon had tried his hand with Siobhan, while McX was on the telephone ruining a life.

In my lord's wood, by their house grown, there is a ruined cottar town. Here in season the Italians stalk their imaginary game, though there are plenty of rabbits. Why come all the way from Rome to kill a rabbit? The sport of it!

Here one day McX rushes from the house after scalding himself making tea. Siobhan thought him ham-fisted and was cross with him; the burn the more painful for that. He used to make tea without bother, under his lamp . . . He sits on the rise of an old foundation and looks about him. It is a clean and dark wood, floored with ferns. What were the floors of the cottars? The smoke of McX's cigarette rises parallel to the trees.

He sits on the corner of what was a *place*. He can see what once were houses. Now only suggestions of lines under leaves. He looks back at the cottage, smoke from the chimney. Thinks of Siobhan going to work in the big house beyond the field. Thinks of her gently stirring a pot on the huge black range, Baudrons the black cat purring beside her, occasionally opening his eyes to see if any of the birds hanging in the cold-press have fallen. Or come to life.

McX hunches, squints, and tries to imagine the life of the cottar town. Smoke in the chimneys now gone. The city here the warrens of the rabbits and the tunnels of foxes. In the sunlight at the edge of the wood, new snares of bright wire shine along the fence.

These snares are set and operated by Grant, his lordship's gamekeeper. Of a night, Grant is fond of pulling at his pint and pipe and saying:

I catched rabbits!

McX sees Grant afar, moving along a fence, checking the snares. His worn gamekeeping jacket bulges with death – rabbit paws stick at angles out of the pockets. Grant looks like a man handing out cigars.

Grant sells the rabbits to Cambeul, butcher in the town. He walks in every Friday afternoon with carrier bags out of which blood is coming. Cambeul pays Grant seventy-five pence for each rabbit. Occasionally Grant attempts to slip in an old tough hare, and is reprimanded in Calvinist tones by Cambeul.

Cambeul's shop is a monument to the hunt, smell, and death. Its front is of pink mortuary granite. Behind windows framed in oak and varnished with an undertaker's care by Cambeul, tilted marble slabs display the unremarkable dead. Slabs equipped with pipes to dispense cooling, freshening water. But around here we don't want things any too fresh.

Cambeul's looks like a grotto where dried monks and skulls live. Pheasants, grouse, rabbits hang from the ceiling, metal hooks through their legs, their eyes open in surprise at every customer. The same animals hang so in every Highland kitchen, one of Siobhan's fears as she grew in Moray.

The taste of rich musty flesh. Not for us the bled flavourless meat of the supermarket. We want to taste death; we see it all about us. You cannae do this with fish, mind, they do not rot nobly, we dinna trust 'em anymore.

On the slabs of Cambeul lie dead kye and rabbits, pigs and deer. Men and women quieten as they walk by, pay their respects to Cambeul's bloody equipment and calling.

McPint will stick his face to Cambeul's window, as he will leer into Smillie's. With the same desire with which he scans the latest

offerings of the pornographers, he will survey
the bound legs of the rabbits, their demure little
feet, their startled look much the same as the
poor flashgun-snared women of *Wow*.

Sitting in the wood McX looks up into the
trees. Their colours the deep green of duck and
grouse wings hanging in the kitchen where
Siobhan works, all the kitchens of Scotland. It
has become dark, it will rain, though there are
still bright circles on the hills. McX gets up and
walks over the humps of the ruined town,
walking he knows over the city of the rabbits.
The gates to this city are everywhere and McX
can hear the rabbits moving. Some of them are
sick. He knows they are watching him.

Toward the fence, the snares, the open field,
McX sees something bright poking at him from
a rabbit hole. Thinking it is a drink can, left by
an Italian or Wintersgill, he moves to take it up.
McX does not want colours in the wood which
do not belong. It is a rained-on copy of *Wow*,
rolled up.

This frightens McX: some horrific plookie-
face has been out here from the town with a
copy of *Wow*. McX searches for other traces of
debauchery – fag ends, a whisky bottle? Nothing. A wanker has *been* here, at night? with a
torch? and what is worse, within sight of McX's
bedroom window, the bedroom he shares with
Siobhan. McX reddens and sweats as the idea
of McPint in the night wood comes to him.

Briefly, continuing on, he imagines rabbits

looking at *Wow* as men look at rabbits in Cambeul's.

Wow is soggy, hell knows from what. McX tries to thumb through – a hint of flesh here and there – but it is like trying to thumb through pancakes. Mortified and uneasy he continues toward the fence. Raining now.

At the edge of the wood there is a rabbit not dead in a snare. If only that were McPint. The ditch running between the fence and the field is filling with rainwater. Under the scattered shelter of a tree McX lights a cigarette to consider the ditch problem. The idea that smoking a cigarette will give you information – !

From the road, a slugging noise: Wintersgill in a battered Land Rover. He has stopped to right a post, his job, there is nothing to be done, all is mud and vexation of spirit.

The rain comes harder. McX does not want Wintersgill to see him emerge from the loved wood with a men's magazine, pulpy as it may be. The only thing: put it back in a rabbit hole. And does, watched by the rabbit jerking in the snare.

McX turns still smoking and nervous, wild, and tries to bridge the ditch. With his nicotine-weak limbs he goes right in, up to his knees.

I must get back to my pipe!

He drops his cigarette in the water and begins to work his way out of the suctioning muck. Pulls himself up onto the sticky field. Breath comes hard in Scottish rain.

Say you! Wintersgill calls from the road. He cups his hands: Why don't you get a motor car?

McX makes a movement like pushing Wintersgill away, down. He walks toward the cottage, directly across the field. The kye sit with their hopeless rain-look, they do not come over. As McX looks at the smoke coming out of his chimney, the scald throbs on his hand. Have to return to that hurt inside.

Is there nothing to do but wrestle with the damn weather?

Somewhere in Scotland a rat is gnawing. Rat of history, rat of night. Gnaw, crunch – !

McX is awakened agonizingly by tiny shakes from Siobhan. From an hibernatory sleep in the first night of winter snow, it is weary miles to consciousness of the bedroom. The faintest of lights from the loyal moon, dimmed by busy clouds.

What is it!

Listen!

Scrape! Crack! That thing is trying to get in here. It is eating stone. Wintersgill has told of battalions of rats he has seen, emigrating, stealthy, on dark dark nights. The worst thing that ever can be seen in your headlamps, worse than a hundred rabbits you know your motor car must strike, worse than sudden black ice, worse than a human body. A moving field of

rats, the ground seething, the whole history of
Europe and the humiliations of Scotland. Rats!

It's not funny, it's coming for us, squeaks
Siobhan.

She knows it is not only the rat coming but
the moon and every dead animal she has ever
seen, all her own ghosts, the Grim Reaper, a
black bull's head and all the House of Hanover.
Siobhan's voice is thin with anger, with historical resentment that McX is not already up and
killing.

McX puts on a tired dromedary robe and
processes bleary to the back door. Still in sleep,
through his natural thickness he thinks: a rat is
just outside. It is trying to eat the metal
weather-strip, it is so hungry. McX leans his
head on the jamb and thinks about hunger,
about his possible kinship with the brown
desperation outside. Brown disgust.

Do something! a cry from the bedroom.

McX kicks his bare foot against the door and
pounds on the wood below the glass – Roar! –
snarls and yells. Loud, foolish.

The rat stops for the briefest time. It must be
mad with lust, insane for warmth and food.
McX is frightened by the short pause. Here a
real adversary. Nightmare. Why him, in his
peaceful cottage which Siobhan has decorated,
why a rat come to tear it apart with teeth? A
rat angrier than his lordship, with teeth
sharper than McX ever wished he had when
angry, wanting to tear up and bloody the

miserable world.

To the fireplace. Obeisance to the household god. Grasps the heavy poker. Fortunately a big old one for wood, none of your good-luck-horseshoe six-inch ones for citified fires – this is a real clobberer with a curved vicious toenail . . .

Hurry! from the bedroom.

All right!

McX is sickened – the urgency of Siobhan tells him he is being tested. Siobhan of the hills and creatures, why are you putting and pitting me this way? The cottage goes from castle to cave.

McX at the door, the rat going crazy. McX: Roar! He bangs on the door, clatters the knob and the metal strip with the poker.

Don't make marks! from the bedroom.

Shut the hell up!

McX wishes he were wearing shoes. He undoes the catch and seizing the knob flings the door open: Roar!

The – rat – is – very – large. So big that McX unhunches his organs and screams bloody murder and slams the door, leaning, panting, harrowing himself with the eyes of the thing: calculating, mad. The rat starts in on the door again.

Could have taken ma whole leg aff!

What's the *matter* with you? Why haven't you killed it?

Too fast for me!

Huh!

Siobhan is now in the back hall in her silk dressing gown, the peach cast-off of an old Glaswegian lady. Long dead.

Why don't you do something?

McX squints and breathes heavy. I must get back to my pipe.

Poison, he says.

Poison! It'll eat us before it eats poison!

McX strides manly to the pantry. He swings the poker general-like as he goes. He rummages, for poison. Breaks up the horrid green cake. Wants to eat it. Puts it on a plate.

That's a good plate, what are you thinking of?

Oot the way!

He makes for the door. Siobhan flees to the bedroom. McX flashes the outdoor light on and off, bangs the poker on the door – Roar! – rattles the knob and whips the door open. The rat jumps back a foot. It sneers at McX and advances three inches. McX slams the door behind him, O God good thing his toes are hidden in the snow. The rat dances back and forth, McX slashes at it with the poker which clangs muffled on the flags. The rat is brave and crazy, it howls and hisses at McX who hurtles the poker to one side and then the other of it. It occurs to him he cannot bring the curved black spike down on the thing itself, fegs no. Roar! The rat screams and suddenly runs away, making for the space under McX's shed. My lord's revenge? Breathing in the sharp snow air

McX walks to the shed, puts down the poison plate just before it, expecting his hands and feet to be bit off in a trice. He turns and walks toward the house in a narrow tunnel of light, Siobhan at the bedroom window. McX strides in his robe, swings the poker, wants to scream, wants to run. He opens and closes and bars the door. Stands with chest heaving in the little hall, staring at an old flour tin and a bottle of Siobhan's bramble wine.

Replaces the poker on the fireplace and bows once again, inwardly.

Hum the *Siegfried Idyll.* McX enters the bedroom slowly in the dromedary robe. Siobhan is standing at the window, her chestnut hair down, draped like the dead lady's silk robe. McX stands next her. In the light from their window they see the rat rush from under the shed to the plate. It snaps up the cake and begins staggering about.

I've hurt you, little brother, and I am glad.

Silently they go to bed and put out the light. It doesn't seem to be any time of the night at all. It occurs to McX they are silent because Siobhan is not speaking to him. He reaches for her. She is stiff.

What's the matter noo?

What a palaver you made of that.

Here the hero lies in his bed with no thanks. It's a brave man shows his fears. But och, what of it? What would Prince Charlie have done? Pranced about in his kilt and run away to raise

help by subscription. What would Wallace have
done? Would have tried to live with it and it
would have sold him out. Robert the Bruce?
Would have stabbed it and never let you forget
it. Cluny MacPherson? Would have eaten it.
Keir Hardie? Nationalized it. McPint? Screwed
it. Would any of these have rid Scotland of this
rat to Siobhan's satisfaction?

McX wanted Siobhan in his moment of
triumph. He lies half turned from her, feeling
weak.

She doesna like me, she doesna like me.

GUY FAWKES NIGHT

There is Siobhan and the moon, and there is
McX and Siobhan and the moon and the bridge.
A humped bridge far out in the fields, away
from his lordship's castle, away from the cottage, away from the road. Under the bridge
there is an earnest eddy, always embracing the
same round stone and the same triangular
stone.

Siobhan and the moon are friends. Well – the
moon is friendly toward Siobhan, and for the
moon Siobhan has the love of fear. When she
feels her most tender to the hills and birds and
weather, she will step out with the moon and
share a cigarette with it, both of them wreathed

with haze: any thing of value in Scotland is haloed. The moon, loved ones who smoke, the blur of one's qualities, mountains, the sea of the Hebrides.

On a night without rain or sleet, when McX and Siobhan gaze at each other in the after-supper mirror, where besides ideas of love they see a call to the fields, they will go together to the bridge. At the night bridge McX feels the whole of his love for Siobhan, the moonlight, the wellies she has given him, the shirt he has chosen to wear because of her, her hair and the wind. At the bridge his eyes unhood, his back straightens, he is barely McX, hardly Scottish.

The bridge is the only place where Siobhan speaks whole, of the moon, her land. The bridge is to her mind as is the cottage mirror to their love-making. Siobhan sees and thinks, she says, most clearly at the bridge under the moon.

Siobhan studies McX, the dromedary curve, its relation to the lines on his face; studies his hand with cigarette, his clothes which have changed and become earnest since they two came together in the cottage. She sees how much she has given him, and realizes out of how much love this has been. She had hoped merely to use McX as they use the mirror over their beloved mantel: she expected no invasion from a man that is such a Frankenstein of others' parts. Now she becomes afraid: all the fears she learned, that were her self, the bottling of secret loves, forsaking, denying the

love of men and women, all her journey from
the singing other-music life of Moray, all these
ghosts have begun to slip away from her now.
And she can't have it. Without them she will be
alone, nothing. By herself.

In the mist the beginning of rejection. Of
resignation.

McX's eyes are shining with love and, since
they have left the mirror but recently, desire for
Siobhan and Siobhan alone. There may be
several lights there, but each is the beacon of a
different regard for her. McX loves at the same
moment the whole of her, her skin, a memory
he has of her walking up a street in Kirriemuir,
and especially her nobility, her grace, her
hands. And he is loving Blackwood.

Siobhan knows nothing of Blackwood, yet she
sees that important light signalling on the coast
of McX. She begins to despair and even to hate.
It is not right. She cannot breathe, she feels
caged. How could she know she is loved
through an imaginary child, without being told?
Yet such is one of the ways to love.

For McX too the moonlight is a truth-giver.
He sees Siobhan's doubts and fear: what could it
possibly be that is wrong? He becomes troubled,
suddenly taken aback by the complicated way
he loves her.

But there is always time for hollow gaiety.
The mist is thickening along with McX's disquiet. Through it he can make out the small
colourful lights of sparklers and fireworks at

the castle. He pictures my lord staggering about, Roman candle in hand, giving orders, setting pets afire. In front of invisible cottages about the fields are sprightly wee flames and showers of light: the Guy who tried to blow up the English parliament is worth a match or two and a toast tonight oh aye. Penny for the Guy? Have a pound. And have a dram. My love is like a red red fuse.

Silent Siobhan and McX walk slowly up the brae from the burn to their cottage. Where their eyes meet are the beginnings of storms. McX, full of fear and hollow gaiety, bundles Siobhan into a heavier coat. November is not a joke at night. From behind the press he extracts his sack of little treats: a sparse kit of fireworks and a bottle of whisky. Siobhan is touched: a memory of her grandfather dutifully setting off a single Catherine wheel in the middle of his Calvinist night.

Siobhan and McX in dark fog with a bottle of whisky and a box of explosives: they cannot see their house. McX pads back and forth in the vegetable patch lighting the fireworks, all of which are the same, wan highway flares. In the gaseous light of them he pulls Siobhan close, thrilled by the feeling of her in her coat of artificial animal. He kisses her eyes which dance from the fireworks and tears of hollow gaiety.

She has slipped away, she has left herself at the bridge, where she prefers to remain with

her self and her ghosts, where she wants only
to remember loving McX. She cannot think of
lying next him now. She trembles, he hopes it
is with cold; he kisses her and it is bitter.

Siobhan manages to smile. It is the smile of
resignation she learned long ago at the
graveyard yett, in dark corners waiting for her
lover, a smile she taught herself when crying
on her bed of girlhood. She smiles and her eyes
are wet.

McX goes to bed without her this Guy Fawkes
Night, much as he wants her there. He is brave:
his spirit has expanded so under the moon and
whisky mist, with the male love of sulphur, that
he tells himself she wants to be with the moon
for a time. Of all her lovers this is the one of
which he should be jealous!

McX broils slowly on his blanket for a time
and goes to sleep. Someone might add leeks
and onions under the bedclothes and make him
into a crispy bake.

Blackwood is his dream when they are happy,
Hephzibah when they are not.

Five miles from town is a place quite dear to
McX. Having visited it once or twice, he often
goes there in dream. It is a vale sheltered by old
oaks and by the more modern windbreaks of
farms. Streams wander through, under miniature footbridges, over casual little dams and

through abandoned weirs. Decrepit cottages look out from behind flowering bushes. This place has the enclosed cosiness of a stage set, a crazy-golf park; the strange comfort offered to the insane by cute areas or systems, miniature villages, dioramas, cog railways, England.

On a rise at the top of the field is a castle, fine and tall. Two slender towers, joined late in life, after threats had passed from the minds of men who lived in castles.

A famous leap by a famous lass between the towers saved her from being found in the arms of: a churl, in someone's opinion anyway.

McX pays the ticket mannie who drowses over his machine. In the cool hall, on the remnants of a painted ceiling, flowers dogs men and bears march in rich colours along black rafters.

McX climbs up into a turret. His shoulders hunch and his chest caves in. Smoke? Better bloody hell not. Ancient monument. I must get back to my pipe. He peers out a slit, imagines peering fearfully out, to see a line of enemy helmets and halberds appear suddenly at the bottom of the field. On the narrow stair of danger in the past, the slit offers little reassurance: it is five or six times the width of an arrow. To look out and see *enemies* coming, intent on getting in your castle and chasing you up and down stairs and then stabbing you right through to the cold stone floor! Imagine the sound, the feel to stobber and stobbee. McX inhales quickly and squints his eyes as if smoking.

Suddenly my lord's daughter Hephzibah is with him on the turret stair. She faces him, her back to the slit. Hephzibah inclines her aristocratic jaw in an invitation to kiss, the narrow strip of historic landscape behind her giving great contour to her artistically modelled features.

McX's fingers open in imaginary drop of imaginary cigarette which with a little twist of toe he imaginatively crushes oot. He moves to her, pulls the heraldry of her garments and the flesh of her to him. His corduroy dromedary mingles sluggishly with her tailored country look. Leaning his jaw on her shoulder McX looks out the slit loving to dream in dream and good God

sees his lordship fuming up the field like a locomotive, knocking down the ticket mannie. Another rasp of breath – McX grasps Hephzibah's shoulders and points out the slit.

Even without armour my lord is a formidable enemy. Hephzibah slips down the stair. McX ascends to the roof, a classic tactical mistake. His lordship may be heard below in the great hall.

Where the hell is that fucking bastard? Get out of my way you little hairie!

Hephzibah protests in high semiquaver but cannot bar the way. Storm of titled sozzled footsteps on the stair.

Why I'll – !

McX at the edge of the leaded roof, his foot on the crenellation. At the base of the tower, angry thistles wait to cradle him. Balloo, ballaa. Footsteps. For a moment McX is paralysed, caught, ruthven from head to toe. Then shapeless and strained as an early flying machine he leaps, historical, across to the other tower and dives into its turret, hurrying down the stair. I must get back to my pipe.

Hurtles across the field, across the road, along a winding path, having himself now knocked down the poor wee ticket mannie, breaking his machine, spilling his Err-Na-More in the long grass.

From the castle: imprecation upon imprecation, followed by a screech of lordly tyre.

Finding himself most dreadfully in the open, McX dives into one of the disused weirs. Struggles in the winter water to remove his shoes, floats close to the old concrete wall. An unutterable feeling, naked toes against green brown mossy mossy. What fish might come?

An opulent motor car speeds along the path over McX's wet head dromedary coat and of course cigarettes. He soaks until he is sure the motor will not return. A green door opens in one of the crazy-golf cottages and a mannie in a worn official cap wanders down to the water, a worn official dog with him. The *weir-keeper*, of all things.

Ye cannae stay in there all day.

I can pay you, says McX, I've got money.

An unknowable hour in the dark narrow Scotland of the Night which has filled McX's brain and bed. Some motion, and he wakes to find Siobhan is next him. He half turns to her, as he always wishes to do, and finds this is not Siobhan who is always cool as the linen, not Siobhan who brings Highland shadows to their bed. She is feverish and clammy; if she weren't so chill McX might almost think he lay next to himself roasting on the blanket. Siobhan turns and twists in a way he has never seen nor imagined she could.

It's me, says McX. All right?

Siobhan cannot hear him. She is turning, turning, she is wet: perspiration and tears.

What's the matter!

Don't!

Siobhan shakes, heaves like a small animal with a disease. Perspires: *gin.*

McX turns from her, his eyes wide and shoulders hunched in bewilderment. He is chastened and deeply frightened. Siobhan reeks of many moonlight cigarettes, sherry and gin. McX imagines her lying in front of the fireplace or reeling about the kitchen she loves... Siobhan smells like *McPint.* McX begins to weep.

Turfed out, that's what. McX stands and smokes on the broken concrete step of the cottage, looking across the fields to the wood, toward his lordship's crabbed castle. Here in this house, among these trees, in these fields, here in the snow and muck which down inside him he loves, life isn't possible? Love is condemned to be a Scotsman?

All the Scots are down in hell, swaying back and forth, even the ticket mannie, crying out, 'Forgive us, Lord, we didna ken, we didna ken!' And the Lord in Heaven looks over the edge of his throne and says, 'Well – ye ken it noo!'

The kye come over to the fence to investigate the humped and smoking object which stares back at them. No happiness here. Not among trees this pretty or in the geometric spaces between McX's shed and the cottage and the old byre. Of course not. Might have known.

A scrabbling noise and a whimper. From the hedge that runs alongside the ditch comes a rabbit far gone in myxomatosis, its eyes dead pink balls. A little legacy from my lord, through the agency of Wintersgill and Grant. McX smokes and stares, helpless, at the myxie rabbit. It sits, twitching, heaving its sides, and crying. Trying to see. When he was in the security, the warm bag of the Highland pipes of love, McX would have got a shovel and smashed! the life out of this poor thing, out of charity. Now he stands and watches the rabbit try to look at him, try to sense the cottage. McX turns and looks into the windows. The nautilus will have to leave his shell altogether. Love died in those rooms, strangled by he knows not what, killed by something wrong, or secret, love dead of apnoea.

It is too much, all that hurt in there and outside this creature heaving in agony.

Clouds flee their maker across the hills towards McX and the dying rabbit.

Poor rabbit, poor McX. Poor old Scotland.

IV

THE WORD EDINBURGH

Whoever hath once seen Edinburgh, with its couchant crag-lion, will see it again in their dreams.

Charlotte Brontë

If one doesn't care for dreams, one doesn't care for typography – it is a dreamy idea. Arriving in boldly cut, soar-glassed Waverley after your long journey, there is both thrill and peace to be had in contemplation of the word E D I N B U R G H in dim sun from above.

In high letters, perhaps gently curving art deco from the shade pen of Mackintosh, the word Edinburgh is tall and lovely as Ramsay Garden, and the tall lands peopling, soldiering up the rift toward the Castle; the loops and kerns at the top of such a face the turrets and happy narrow windows of those celebrating houses.

Tall as Ramsay Garden, squat as Waverley or Leith. Even Helvetica the heartless, curse of the age, cannot entirely relieve the word Edin-burgh of its nobility.

In the extended letters of railway carriages, in the delicate lettering of the taxicab door the word Edinburgh sings the city. In paint or leaf or forged iron it comes as a boon and a blessing to men. The word Edinburgh flies banners from its own spikes and vanes, contains all its steps passages and closes. Leaves in the word Edin-burgh catch the sun and the rain. The word is grey and strong as the Castle rock, the lift of Arthur's Seat, the towers and turrets of Holyrood. Through the iron bars of the word Edinburgh may be glimpsed the headstones of Greyfriars, and through it runs the Water of Leith.

Capital R, capital of Scotland. Roman R, the Roman law of Edinburgh, foundation of the law of Scotland. Set in Century, set in the centuries. Set in Didot, the Auld Alliance.

The ways it is spoken. The *Edinbrah* of the English train announcer. The plooman's *Embro*. The Frenchman's pretty *Edimbourg*. Umbrellas join macintoshes in the rain of Princes Street.

The proud way it is rightly said, a word of perfect hard and soft, the rhythm and strength of a Strathspey: a perfect practice of Scottish rhythm, of sad song coming and going in the life of Scotland with her moving clouds. The word Edinburgh could be played all day on a violin.

The burr of the burgh the curl of the turret's lightning-rod, the little barb of Scottish endings, antlers in Highland halls. The E of Edinburgh the national standard, in a spirit-safe, for pronunciation of the Scottish E. None of your English iiihs or eeks.

The word Edinburgh displays the full life and meaning of the city. Its effect on the English-speaking eye is at once familiar and foreign. The nobility of the word is well shown in Gill, and it appears in this fount in many places about the city. The word Edinburgh is a perfect portrait of the noblest city of Britain.

Wherever you go, write the word Edinburgh on any convenient paper, so that your eye may always find a home. Glance at it at odd times as you might at the portrait of a friend.

As the word contains the city, so the city contains all of Scotland, at once delicate, grand, bold, crude, rich, poor, natural and artistic. Stand in Princes Street on a day of sun and cloud and say you don't see pride and humility, faith and the profane, music and noise, learning and oatmeal, beauty and squalor, a nation's history and its wretched decline into piddling commerce each trying to kill the other.

In between the shadows and glimmers, the line and curl of this word, is all this country: McX's town and the mud of his ditch, what he finds among twigs, Siobhan and her childhood, McPint and his fag ends and smashed glasses of beer.

Great northern metropolis! Where men's noses are inflamed dripping penises, where girls shatter like floury china at your touch, where fresh fruit is regarded with only the deepest suspicion.

It is McPint walking in sunshine dim and early. With his hair sticking out, his cheeks unshaved, his night breath rasping in his throat,

McPint sandpapers the air of the city as he walks through it.

McPint has no destination in mind. His brain is sore. It drove him from his bed. There is a man in it. He is unaware of his route.

Stimulated by the smell of boiling hops in the Canongate, he wanders up and down it. Bumps and dings into posts, doorways, like a bearing in a pinball machine – invisible things, scenes of ancient riot, houses that no longer exist, places where men were hanged.

? something happens to make him realize he has arrived at the Black Ox. He finds himself staring at its dark windows. There is a thing new and bright to behold in them: *Go-Go Dancer – Lunchtimes,* in fluorescent orange. Scales fall from McPint's eyes. He is truly awake.

Now the day takes on meaning. *Now* there is something to think about: what to do between now and then. Then! when he will, he can already imagine, feast the red and ferocious McPint eye on a half-naked gyratrix.

McPint feels heat in his groin. He looks over his shoulder to see if anyone is about and then, via his pocket, adjusts his genital.

McPint treats time like bog roll. Four hours to murder. Their cruel end is like this: on down the Canongate goes McPint. In a newsagent's he peruses *Wow* until told to get out. A piss in the toilet of the brewery wall. Down to the bottom: Holyrood. Stands in the forecourt and stares, briefly intrigued by the conical turrets of lead.

McPint stumbles around the ruined abbey. He tries to read tombs, cranes his neck painfully, slowly perceives it used to be a building, eh like a church. McPint accosts a guide.

What happened to this place then, eh?

Burnt down, Sir.

When?

Och, a long time ago.

Long time ago stirs McPint's brose of a memory. Something, a name, comes up.

Cromwell?

The guide sees McPint is severely hung over, that he is hung over and nationalistic; he wants an answer, a simple *answer*. Injustice surges out of the mild little guide, tears well up in his eyes:

Aye, Oliver Cromwell's the man responsible for that, Sir!

McPint, satisfied, falls over a tomb and is helped up.

In the forecourt once again, McPint reflects on history. Farts, intermittently. He sees, passing by the far gate, McX, who is trying to make his way along the street but is caught up in a gathering crowd of some kind. McPint goes after him, emitting a wisecrack and another fart.

Oh, it's you, says McX. Aye.

What you doing around here then?

McX holds up his clinical case.

You here to test the Queen's whisky?

Ha. Across the road.

But McPint and McX are now nearly im-
mobile with thronging. McX's round corners
enable him to lever himself about and enquire.

What's the idea?

It's the Queen ya eejit, says a toothy girl, she's
comin oot in a minute!

McX feels a little thrill. He looks down at the
crown embossed on his case, re-hunches his
corduroy, assumes an air of importance. He
imagines being the Weights and Measures to
the Royal Household, the Queen's gauger,
chained to the gates of Holyrood so as to be
available at any time things need measured.

What about a glass of beer? says McPint.

Don't you want to see the Queen?

Ach, spits McPint, she's no *my* fuckin Queen!

A gentleman turns to look at him:

Here, Sir, perhaps you've never heard of the
Act of Union?

Heard of it! says McPint, I've *done* it!

Now now, says McX, he doesnae mean that.

And it's a hell of a lot more excitin than
hangin aboot here waitin for that bitch, says
McPint.

In the joy of having a captive audience McPint
begins to denounce the houses of Hanover and
Saxe-Coburg. Sellers-oot, the deaths of us all.

To the King over the water! yells McPint. He
jumps back and forth across a little unsavoury
puddle on the ground.

I'll tell you what about Charles Edward
Stuart, says McX. I read it in a book that after
he left us he went to Rome and became a *'drink-
sodden voluptuary'*.

McPint stops hopping.

Ach, nice work if you can get it, says McPint,
the aristocrats have all the advantage.

How red in the face McPint gets. How the idea
of the Queen shakes the bones in the tombs of
his forebears. Though McPint has no ancestors
being a very true real bastard. The imminent
appearance of Her Majesty has McPint foaming
at the mouth, a beard of froth forms round his
neck. He looks like Keir Hardie.

A black car pokes at the crowd, a pastel hat
behind the glass. The crowd sighs like spring-
time, and here is McPint jumping up and down!
His bonnet in the air again and again, Hooray!
Hooray! Hooray! As the most exuberant member of the crowd he attracts the attention of the
Duke, who waves. McPint is ecstatic!

Did ye see that? he cries in a high voice, that
was the *Duke* of *Edinburgh*, he waved at me!

McPint's eyes shine like a boy's. His life may
be complete.

McPint and McX find a pub in the Canongate.
After his second pint of 80/- McPint belches.

She wasnae a bad-looking bit, in the war.
Used to wear fetchin wee hats and that. There
was a little grey one –

You mean, says McX, you fancy the Queen?

Ach, says McPint flushing, she's a bloody

German, McX. Just remember that.

McPint's skin begins to crawl in the clammy sun of noon. He is nearing the Black Ox. *Go-Go Dancer – Lunchtimes.* Why hasn't he, as a premium customer, been informed?

He imagines what oiled kind of temptress would dance go go for the delectation of the Black Ox. She will dance in a cage, there will be throbbing lavender stroboscopic light and wild discorotic music, featuring snorting and slobbering. *Just like in Aberdeen.*

McPint begins to salivate. He hies into view of the Black Ox, the orange rectangle. He pauses at the door and licks his lips.

He enters to find the place stuffed with funny-looking men, men he has never seen before. They all look like postmen, their suits baggy and dark, they are undernourished all, unshaven and ashamed. These men are all standing there. With the same stoop of shoulder and the same glass of beer. Silence, layers of smoke – are they waiting for a strike vote? The news of a bomb?

McPint makes his way to the bar. Pint of 80/-! Without drinking he gingerly uses his glass as a periscope: a plywood box in front of the jukebox, a red reflector bulb trained on it through the smoke. Eyes steal up toward the clock. It is a minute past the appointed time.

Heat, sweat. Dust? Yippie ki yi yo.

The door of the women's bog opens. And she comes out. The men shift uneasily.

She is short and has Siamese cat eyes. She is wearing whay you might expect, some St-Tropez drug addict's idea of the lower-torso heritage of the Navajo, with a towel draped round her shoulders.

She is dark, McPint thinks. He thinks: she is a tink. Aye a beautiful tink named Fiona.

Slowly Fiona puts some coins into the jukebox. She stands on the plywood box and puts her towel off. The perspiring barman cranks up the red bulb. She stands preprofessionally, she's been to dancing school. The men stand unprofessionally, they've never been anywhere. Well – some of them have been on the rigs, what pass today for India.

Start of thump-music. She raises her arms over her head, lowers her eyes in TV passion –

and *now* the conversation begins, loudly. To a man they all turn away from her! Suddenly! In unison! Stridently croaking out hastily invented talk of golf, sport, motor cars. Having all crowded in! Not a single one is brave enough to look at her now, grasping her ankles, moving her bottom back and forth, displaying a demarcation of demaquillation alas and alack.

McPint is the only one looking. He is facing her and two hundred men are facing him – two hundred postmen staring through him or perhaps trying to see the reflection of what she is doing in McPint's eyeballs.

The pint was dear: McPint feels bound to watch, but they're all looking at him – *he* feels on stage.

Her attitudes are few in number. Invites you to her breasts, demonstrates the line of her torso as if she is the latest refrigerator, bottom of breast to thorax. Wraps one leg around air as though you or some extension of you. Now bends, is being had by not you, too violent, some muscular bloke in threatening underwear from Empire Stores. And begins again.

McPint blushes salmon. Struggles upstream against the faces. He can hardly hear the music for the chatter. He cools his face in his glass: hiss!: looks again: wow: hiss!: wow: hiss!

The coins run out. The red bulb dims immediately. No applause. She is red in the face. With moist brow and lip she takes the towel, mopping herself like a boxer, in the once again dead hot silence she trips into the toilet, the pasteboard door of which shuts: ka-ponk.

Expensive embarrassment. McPint furiously gulps the rest of his 80/- which is hot in his hand.

Another!

In twenty minutes' time she (according to the orange rectangle) will come out and grasp her ankles again. What's she going to do for all that time? Sit on the bog? Laugh at them all? Cry her eyes out?

SECRET SCOTSMAN

The city of Edinburgh is a salubrious abode for
the secretive personality. Who keeps himself to
himself, and from himself, quickly finds a
companion in this warrened, wynded, staired
place which discloses its delights and shames
only when it knows you. And then by accident,
by slow degree.

The secret soul may take a particular interest
and pleasure in *creeping,* the method of which
may be learnt from old films. To creep, under
cover of night or mist, is a thrilling way to get
about. Chance encounters and pre-existing
appointments are charged with greater interest, with piquancy, if one has crept there,
close to a wall with hand outstretched or a
sleeve obscuring the face.

Creeping of a superior sort may be accom-
plished in Advocates Close, a frightening
haunted valley, in Lady Stair's Close, mist
hanging on its corbie-steps, turrets and lamps,
or down Castle Wynd to the Grassmarket,
mysterious and ugly. Truly horrifying creeping
may be done under the bridges and along the
Cowgate, but here other creepers may be
encountered, creepers who creep for reasons
beyond pastime.

Creeping is a reasonable way of defying authority. A policeman might apprehend you creeping, but in the absence of any evidence of wrongdoing in the vicinity, what charge could be brought?

Wasting police time. Method: creeping.

But you have nettled them. Even when they are invisible. To creep is to give yourself importance, to assert the complexity of human life against the impassivity of the elements. What better demonstration to the sun, the moon, the Castle, the vapours and forbidding stones of a gigantic city, that you are not as small and simple as you look?

On a day thick with fog and coal smoke Totemic Smith chooses, after creeping along Kings Stables Road, haunting the Grassmarket sight unseen, even though it is mid-morning, to creep up Castle Wynd with his hand stretched out, crabbed, following slowly up the steps, through broken bottles and pools of the urine of several species.

The Castle only barely sensible, a stern thing behind clouds. Before landing on Castlehill he passes: an inert man, a terrier so cold Totemic Smith sees it decide not to bite him, a man in a bus-driver's uniform and a hairie called China Pig in congress. His ticket machine has dropped to the stone step, she is wearing his cap. They too decide not to bite him.

Arrival of Totemic Smith on Lawnmarket. Dim, behind a whole library of fogs, dejected

blue banners droop over the portal of the
Castle, an intriguing arch beyond which there
might just as well be empty space.

A pin-point of light moves like a will o' the
wisp, at certain intervals up and down, the
brakeman's lamp on a dreadful train disappear-
ing forever in swirling haar. It is the cigarette
of Totemic Smith. Totemic Smith outlined, im-
passive against the resonant grey.

What is totemic about Totemic Smith? He is
large, rumpled, friendly, cynical, bearish, sometimes crapulous. Since he is large, he is a totem.
The wee, the punks, can find goodness in the
large people and issues of the world. Though
not all of them have goodness.

Totemic Smith's traditional brogues are size
12. They hark back to the more ancient qualities. Totemic Smith is a declaimer of poetry in
Scots. He has been ejected from drinking-shops
for this. Totemic Smith is a Communist, Totemic Smith is an artist. All day every day with
most of the day a hangover in a metal shed in
Oxgangs he besieges canvas. Perhaps here is
cruel, in a rage to extirpate the city of the night
before.

Totemic Smith is not liked by gallery women.
He falls down too much at his openings. But
isn't that where we all fall down? This is not
important as long as he can purchase Err-Na-
More, coffee-syrup, 80/- and paints, which he
manages to do, just.

On the canvases of Totemic Smith, as McPint

has discovered to his pain and derangement, Clyde steamers have legs to march on and mouths to play bagpipes made of crisp wrappers and whisky-bottles: Dundee shop-girls who would titillate McPint alone, their skirts pulled up and their make-up smudged, are ravished by big nuclear submarines on the steep steep side of Ben Lomond in a dream of heather: wee ticket mannies agape in fear are attacked by lurching churl-shouldered men wearing joke-shop masks of the Prime Minister: black clouds boil in the skies of Totemic Smith, on the misty horizon the fog-mannie has made: rusting shipyard cranes hang and falcon-like beaks of beer-fonts brood: Englishmen are burnt at stakes and Charles Edward Stuart looks on from the summit of Ben Vrackie: blood streams from under his kilt, his sporran stuffed with American money.

Totemic Smith fades from the street corner, where the only proof of life has been the rumble of what sound like taxicabs. He appears in an old building and follows up a dark spiral stair. Green enamel.

To live and wander long enough in fog is to shuck your corporeality, Totemic Smith says as he climbs. In vapour, citizens of this city may freely mix with its ghosts, many of whom are distinguished and historical figures, especially on misty days. Of which there are many.

Totemic Smith emerges into the fog again on the roof. He can make out a wee mannie

in a faded uniform with a ticket machine round
his neck.

This way, Sir, that's fifty pence. Good morning, Sir. Thanking you!

Totemic Smith enters a humped black turret.
Inside, a round white screen on which he looks
down from a balcony.

He comes here most days.

The wee mannie shuts the door behind him.

How are you the day, Sir?

Not so bad!

The mannie turns off the lights and pulls an
old brass lever. Above them an iron iris
squeaks, opens – a shaft of grey light falls on
the screen, mist comes in and swirls around. On
the screen a murky suggestion of the Castle,
hiding . . .

Welcome to Edinburgh – ahem! – Athens of
the North, says the mannie, and as the poet said,
precipitous –

Stuff that muck, says Totemic Smith.

Sir?

It's only me. You know me.

I do aye.

I don't want the tour.

I have to give the lecture, Sir. It wouldna be
right.

Totemic Smith gives the mannie a *pound*!

For your trouble.

Och well, all right Sir. Seeing as it's you. But
dinna tell anybody ye came in here and didna
get the history.

I know the fucking history, says Totemic Smith.

That's right, Sir. You do. Now what would ye like to see the day?

Castle Wynd, says Totemic Smith.

Moving his lever the mannie searches with his great lens up and down the steps of Castle Wynd. But China Pig and the bus driver have gone. So has the inert man. And it seems the little dog has died. But what they do find is McPint emerging from the Black Ox and following a girl in a hat.

McPint has a liking for ladies in hats. Unfortunate for him how few are worn. He has newspaper pictures yellowing of years and years of Royal Ascot which excite him still. McPint will follow a woman in a hat for miles. No matter what she looks like. If she's wearing a hat, that's enough for him and he wants her.

McPint is often successful in this obsession. Do women wear hats with an understanding of men like McPint? Or: on the look-out for? Despite his vigorous ugliness *that's a nice hat yer wearin* is often sufficient to get him a bed for the night, after a drink. And never a lass has objected to keeping her chapeau on for him during the shouting.

McPint's interest in hats has been exploited commercially by someone in that sort of business. Toward the rear of a dubious publication McPint found an advertisement for special interest hats. Highest quality, catalogue sent in plain envelope. Feverishly McPint sent £4.00, refundable with first order.

In a week the postie brought a large envelope. McPint locked himself wildly smoking into the bog to examine the contents. He bulged, furious, rampant at what he saw: Easter bonnets of white kid with razor-blade rims, opera hats in patent leather, a wide-brimmed summer hat of studded red crocodile worn by a wanton English rose who pouted.

McPint must order, to hell with the budget. He chose the black opera and with trembling hands estimated the size of the long-suffering Mrs McPint's head. He filled in the form and sent a sweaty postal order to fetch the thing, like a cur. The sub-shame he felt in the sub-post-office: although the name of the place was innocent enough, She-Hats of London, McPint felt all the men and women of the Royal Mail stare suspiciously at him.

London, London, you can get anything in London, McPint told himself. He drank heavily and drooled for a week. He worried about being on such a depraved mailing list. What kind of devils run such a place? He feared they might show on his doorstep, wanting – oh God! But what, he then thought, is the real harm of such an enterprise? Is it the measure of a civilization's *decadence,* or merely its *intricacy*?

A box arrived. McPint bore it in to the long-suffering Mrs McPint, who was flushed that morning with lateness.

What's this?

A present.

She was in such a bad mood this made no impression, although it was a bastard well unusual event.

Aren't you going to open it?

Oh all *right*.

Enormously the wrong moment, but McPint is ever uncontrollable. The anticipation: she unwrapped, opened –

Oh!

She got red and acted rushed.

What is it with hats! she yelled.

Try it on.

It didnae fit, that was all there was to it. Even so McPint was thrilled. He needed Mrs McPint there and then. The hat absorbed, blocked out her specky shoulders, her tired slip; but she was LATE. She began to scold him.

Ye'll have to return it.

It's non-returnable.

What!

It says here, made to order.

You're mad, you're an idiot! How much did this *cost*!

McPint wouldn't tell her, he was ashamed, she had deeply shamed him. McPint ashamed! She saw her chance, she beat her breast, talked of irresponsibility, the price of fossil fuels,

Ethiopia. McPint was full of remorse. He wanted to give her an amount of money, the price of the hat, but he hadn't got it.

He imagined begging on the street.

He was confused, because the idea had welled up in him, as it did from time to time, that marriage was for some kind of private fun. Once in a while. Even his marriage, honest fun, no matter how expensive.

The long-suffering Mrs McPint stormed out in a flustered way McPint had great distaste for. He had a fear that as they grew older Mrs McPint would one day become a little powdered lavender-watered Scotswoman you might see on the train, going frequently to the toilet to apply more rouge, always saying Ooo.

Mrs McPint knows about the other girls and wishes the hat-wearing could be left to them. It messes her hair.

McPint brimmed with horror at himself. He stared out the window: rain. He had suddenly to get some money, pay her so she could buy something. Must make money. He went into town in complete confusion, his stomach churned on the bus, he cried all day, impercept-ibly. He was ashamed of himself and angry with love for his wife.

Once again wearing the heavenly raiment of marriage as if it were a hair-shirt.

Totemic Smith and the mannie watch McPint in the Meadows, following the girl with the hat.

The mannie works the levers.

Nice Edimbourgeoise, says Totemic Smith.

He's weavin a bit, says the mannie.

McPint is weaving, part with 80/-, part with hat infatuation, but most because he is still being driven mad by the idea he is living in Totemic Smith's head, and Totemic Smith in his.

Anything else? says the wee mannie. Time's almost up, Sir.

Take me down Playfair Steps, says Totemic Smith, I've an idea for a painting there.

The mannie throws the levers, they take a crazy-angled stroll up and down the steps. The mist is giving a bit now, there's a girl selling drawings in pastel, some real sunlight on her face, and some on the bright stone of the National Gallery.

Stuff that place, says Totemic Smith,

Leaning on the railings, a familiar round of shoulder. McX. Staring up away toward Calton Hill. He's moving slightly, there's a glint of light on his cheek. He's crying.

Time's up, Sir, really.

NIGHT EDINBURGH

Toll out unceasing, Edinburgh bell of evening.
Toll out my fright, Edinburgh bell of night.

Beer is not always to be found, satisfactory
beer. Totemic Smith moves up Candlemaker
Row. Beer abounds, to the naked eye, but at the
wrong location, the wrong hour, your glass is
filled with tears, noise, blood, history, or the
finings of crime. Therefore correct beer must
be found and in this Totemic Smith is skilled.

It is a blowy cool night. He moves across the
Meadows, away from the centre of the city.
Away and beyond into twilight he walks, passing hundreds of dirty calm public houses as
though they werena there. Totemic Smith passes the time by impersonating for himself
Drunks I Have Known.

He walks such a distance across and along
the city that he finally comes to the ! Taj Mahal.
It glows opalescent in the moonlight.

Ah, says Totemic Smith. Red flockit walls and
pints o lager.

He peruses the offerings, but this is stupid. He
kens what he wants: capsicum, capsicum,
Dominus vobiscum. So hot you drink a pint
after every bite. He appeals to the waiter.

Very very hot! says the waiter.

Aye I ken.

But no starter, *nothing to start,* Sir?

In shame Totemic Smith mumbles, No. The waiter snatches at the utensils, he flings them away in anger.

A pint of your best lager and lime, says Totemic Smith.

The waiter sweeps wine glasses furiously away and goes to chew them up in his mouth in the kitchen.

Totemic Smith breaks up puppadoms and forms them into a tangram. The Cricketarium, a Diorama: Kirk Yetholm village green, three years before. Totemic Smith plants his glass in re-creation of the sun, setting on his moment of triumph. He selects a burnt sliver, the Jamaican bowler. Gloom and despair rage among the team-mates of Totemic Smith.

We were battling for our honour, he tells himself. Our best had gone down and I was next. A bell in the deep-throated clock tower [the pepper mill] began to chime as I raised my bat, oil-sleek Dark Victory.

Totemic Smith's fingers re-enact the crucial moment through the magic of puppadom puppetry. But voices of unrest are coming from the till.

What d'ye mean, *'No?'*

A much worsened for wear McPint is clutching the formica's edge, moving from side to side before the two short priests of the Taj Mahal.

We cannot sell to you, please. You must

go now, please.

Totemic Smith has come in at the end of this;
Kirk Yetholm is packed up and sent back to the
Borders. McPint's brain rearranges his verte-
brae so he is an inch taller. He just manages to
peer over the till. There is value in peering. He
fixes the priest with the McPint eye, the man
shrinks back, it is a terrible thing to behold.

Who made you? says McPint. *Who made you?*

Dramatic pause omnes.

The British. Just remember that.

McPint turns and walks, stately, out of the
great marble chamber, out, away under the
moon of India, to conquer some other subconti-
nent of drink. There is a man in his head. What
if he had known about Mrs McPint and Balajiprasad?

That man's miserable, says Totemic Smith.

He begins to quote bloodied bone-shards of
MacDiarmid.

Totemic Smith conceives his uncle needs
visited. Duly he goes. A vapour-lit maze of
streets built on small hills.

Totemic Smith's uncle is no very well. He's
sick in the heid. He is a native of Bridgeton,
Glasgow, yet he believes he is a St Kildaman.
He thinks he lives on St Kilda. So rede yersel up.

'Hirta', a white bungalow. The door is opened
by a haggard woman.

Hello, Aunt, says Totemic Smith.

She is destroyed; it was never supposed Totemism was integral to the Smith family.

Totemic Smith follows her to a door. She picks up an implement and blows on it, a deep two-toned signal. Totemic Smith gives her an aggrieved look. The voice of an elderly man from within:

Ah! The mail-boat!

He thinks we are the supply-boat *Dunara Castle,* says Totemic Smith's Aunt, try to act accordingly.

I've never been a supply-boat, says Totemic Smith.

In this suburban sitting-room they find a little man of seventy with a white beard, no moustache, a ruined suit of heavy tweed. He is trying to kindle a fire out of peats on the coffee-table.

Dinna worry, it's too damp, says the Aunt lowly.

News from the mainland! Coal! Food! Tobacco! sings the Uncle.

He is delighted to see them through his little spy-glass.

Hello, Uncle, says Totemic Smith.

He notices a chicken walking behind the settee.

What's that chicken doing?

Wheest, it's a *fulmar,* please refer to it as such, says the Aunt.

Fulmar! I could use a meal . . . says the Uncle.

He thinks he has to catch and eat 'em like

they did on St Kilda, explains the Aunt. He
dreams in Gaelic tae.

He does?

The Uncle climbs slowly up on to the settee.
With his glass he peers down the back of it.

A nest! he cries.

He begins to crawl down the other side of the
furniture, paying out a rope.

How is Uncle, Aunt? says Totemic Smith.

Completely by himself.

Ah! [from behind the couch].

[Scuffling.]

Lovely weather, offers Totemic Smith.

The nights are fair drawin in noo, says the
Aunt.

A sharp cry from behind the sofa, and the
unfamiliar sounds of bird-strangle.

I've got you!

Feathers float up and munching is heard.

Isnae he going to cook that? asks Totemic
Smith, annoyed.

Well he cannae get his peats goin you see,
says the Aunt. It's the damp.

By the fire: tea and a shovel-load of commercial dainties. The Aunt of course is glad to see
her nephew. He is someone to distract her from
her lot in life. But as an artist Totemic Smith is
suspicious of the fireside. In Scotland they try to
trick you into sitting by the fire, where you will
doze, after eating fried food and glutinous cake.
Where you will not, can not read dangerous
books or make art.

Or if you manage it, it will be cute fireside art,
postcard kye, you will tie tartan ribbon on the
kittens of the world.

Totemic Smith eats eleven wee sandwiches.
They will be represented visually tomorrow, as
oppressors. But he knows he cannot linger by
the fire, or his art will be destroyed. Cloaked
inside an immense digestive rumble we hear:

I must get along, Aunt.

A dram before ye go!

Och, well.

They sup in the vestibule. The door to St Kilda
opens. An awful stink – the Uncle smokes coal
in his pipe. He stares at Totemic Smith.

Are ye no the factor of McLeod of Dunvegan?

Good-night, Uncle, says Totemic Smith.

Glasses are put down, hawsers thrown, Totemic Smith's whistle sounds – he leaves this little
bay and turns towards the Hebrides.

Rotation of the hour-hand finds him in the
Western Isles, bare and old-fashioned drinking-
shop. He is well-served by quick men in uniforms. There is naught here to distract you from
80/-.

80/-, the colour of old copper and of trench-
rousingly bitter taste. Yet smooth and creamy
like the sea at St Andrews, or better the ocean
boiling beneath Dunnottar, for it laps at death,
scouring the spine and abrading the soul. Some

believe the soul lives in the cortex and not the pulmonary cavity. In even the stoutest, 80/- eventually snaps something, some Tay Bridge of civilization, and anger ill-judgement and wrong thinking result. 80/- is the *primum mobile* of McPint and all men like him. It never makes Totemic Smith mean, for he has not a mean molecule to be excited. There is the question of cruelty to his canvases – and the public – but Totemic Smith eddies in quiet pools off the river in question. He must drink to create the difficulties which keep him there, and keep him in work.

The pints in the Western Isles rocket back, the arms of all in unison. The lilt and crash of life here becomes garish and mad to Totemic Smith, will soon be a painting. The public house stars descend on him.

I have a great hunger, says Totemic Smith, aye a great hunger for life. For tropical seas, Chilean women, chocolate fondue, gritty Futurist lithography, Calvados, poems, sandwiches, byres, fires, oh a great hunger for it I cannae ignore.

Perhaps you have a tapeworm, says the barman.

Back across the city, windy and late with night. Totemic Smith's path is blocked at a certain junction by two reeling figures, who prove to be

McAitchison and his small deafening dog,
Noisette. Figures of controversy.

Sir! My friend! Won't you join us [he indicates
his stupid dog]?

Totemic Smith has only contempt for
McAitchison, haggard and degenerate tool of
imperialism who seeks to atone under the cloak
of art.

All right! says Totemic Smith.

One of those scenes it is hard to remember or
put a name to ensues in the flat of McAitchison,
poor with the atmosphere of dog and damp
book. It is not an exchange of views, but a
tableau, in which McAitchison ties Noisette to a
chair and then stumbles about the room, regularly tripping over the dog, in a melodramatic
search for a bottle he has hid somewhere and
never finds.

A pretend gentleman, McAitchison has some
sort of war record which titillates in shadow. It
is rumoured McAitchison foiled the plot to kill
Hitler, or that Hitler bungled an attempt on
McAitchison. All as may be. On the map and in
capitals that war is over, but it is fought every
day by millions in the bars of Britain.

If McAitchison had done what they say and is
what they think, then we would not know him.
He would live in a brick house with hermetic
glazing and many hedges in Kent, England, the
anonymous headquarters of faded history and
military nocturnal emission. He wouldna be
bumbling around Edinburgh late in the night

with his uncontrollable dog.

How is your work coming along? says McAitchison.

I'm thirsty, says Totemic Smith.

Oh aye – it'll just be – [Crash]. Now where did I – you know, when I was in the Army –

In his chair, Totemic Smith thinks: it's my fun night.

Down Candlemaker Row the wind blows to Totemic Smith the keenings of citizens in the Cowgate. The gate of Greyfriars squeaks and sings. Wha'd pass a screeching graveyard yett at night deserves what he gets. Totemic Smith stops to light a cigarette, and the wind brings him a little symphony of the past and the life of the city: a window or bottle crashes, a child screams, an argument begins, the horn of a motor car honks angrily, a dog howls, the gate groans:

Listen, says Totemic Smith, to all Night Edinburgh, can ye no hear the pipes?

WHO THE DEVIL

In that quarter of the city called Oxgangs, it is a night in a lane of ancient garages and crazed sheds. It is cold. Totemic Smith has stuffed old canvases into obvious cracks something like McX on holiday. Flood-lamps hang from rafters here and there. They illuminate the loose pink curves of China Pig, who tiredly smokes a cigarette and poses without much art.

She is semi-consciously draped in a short skirt over an assortment of totemic junk: a child's army tank, a collection of toy soldiers, a plush Scottie toy, several cases of whisky, a Victorian fireplace of oak Totemic Smith has found, a stolen headstone, tartan bunting, a rusty tin of Err-Na-More.

Totemic Smith at the easel, his large hand clutches brushes and knives. Right-handed, left-brained. A left-brained painter! Scottish legacy.

As this painting takes shape, the tank gets bigger, China Pig smaller, the tartan becomes a border around the canvas edge, and several political borders – the Tweed, France, Korea, the border between men and women.

What about a cup of tea? says China Pig.

Her back is beginning to hurt. Odd, her most-used thing.

Hold on!

Using a fan-brush, Totemic Smith makes a cloud he knows in the Hebrides, of the colours he used for the tartan. Totemic Smith knows tartan. His mother and father are experts in its provenance. Totemic Smith grew up in the rear of Tartan Discount Supply, Leith. He spent his

childhood among Highland brogues made of
plastic and thin little kilts with horrible great
safety pins in them. Aye for the tourists. The
mind of Totemic Smith was punctured by safety
pins long before the rising of the punks.

Totemic Smith works slowly, with his
mother's movements, the same care she uses
when straightening things in her shop or kitting
out Hamish the display dummy. Hamish the
girning, with the nose of chipped plaster. Hamish has the worst toupee in all Edinburgh and
that is saying something. He figures still in
Totemic Smith's dreams. Never speaking but
always there, with his rug and chipped blank
look. When Totemic Smith's parents die, he
plans to bring Hamish to the shed. Hamish
figures as hero in much of his work.

Totemic Smith puts down his brush and
moves toward the electric kettle. His hands are
rough, he realizes it is cold.

Are ye cold? I'll just put on the heat lamp.

A red bulb from Woolies, Totemic Smith's
idea of winter warmth. Last year it was a crate
of heating liniment, there went his grant from
the arts council.

Oh yes please, says China Pig.

She manages a faint smile. She draws a piece
of the bunting around her shoulders, for
warmth slips on her plastic high heels, and goes
over to the kettle. They two gather round it.

She has not looked at the easel, paintings are
all the same to her. But Totemic Smith pays

more than she could make in an alley the night.
All the same she looks Totemic Smith over and
calculates.

How about a go when ye finish?

Totemic Smith studies China Pig through his
thick spectacles and the little mirk of tobacco
smoke about his sandy head, where he keeps
his own constellations. She has modelled for
him many times. He considers her a friend,
though he has a secret interest in her doings up
and down the stairs and closes of Edinburgh.
She is smoking, which is sex. Relation of bones
to lungs to breasts, black the usual colour of her
clothes, the musculature in sexual X-ray. She
has an appealing scrawniness. Hardness. Her
spiky hair is streaked rat-blonde. Totemic
Smith likes her for her hardness, better shown
in her spirit than her body, which is tough but
ultimately frail. Totemic Smith believes in Celtic woman, as he believes in all symbols. She
sells something intimate to eat, but China Pig is
Celt and woman and keeps herself whole. He
wakes from himself and surveys the effect of
the tartan bunting on her. She widens her eyes.

That's quite good. Aye – keep that on just as
it is when we get back to it.

China Pig makes a pout and a wee snort.

It'd be a plaisure. Ah'm freezin. But what
aboot it?

What aboot what?

A wee go. When ye're done.

Oh well. I don't know. It wouldna be good

for my concentration.

Measly bugger!

Look, I'm paying you just the same!

Ah know!

He likes her in the bunting bolt from Tartan Discount Supply. It is consummate with his subject. He imagines Hamish might fancy her.

The kettle boils. Totemic Smith pours tea for China Pig. For himself he fills a mug half of coffee-syrup and half of sterilized cream. China Pig, shivering, sips the tea and studies the painting.

This is sick, ye ken that?

That so?

What does she know about painting anyway?

D'ye get a lot of money for a paintin like that?

Totemic Smith considers: what is a lot of money?

No!

How much like?

Say – three hundred pound.

Three hundred pound, ye bollocker! Do you know how many blokes up against a wall that is?

He doesnae know, but from now on Totemic Smith resolves to measure the value of art in China Pig's way: how many blokes against an alley wall on a freezing Edinburgh night?

We'd best get on. This is going to take a while.

Och well.

In Oxgangs it is now Scotland of the Night, the yellow vapour wind claws at the shed. Or is it something else – a man – it is, rattling at the door and now hammering.

What the hell, says Totemic Smith putting down his brush.

He opens the metal door, the wind scrapes in and shaves him. In the dark are little white eyes, set far back in the deep red glow of a face. The man stares at Totemic Smith, his eyes shoot past to the light where China Pig pulls her bunting round her.

Ooo!

Hairie though she is, there is a little lavender-watered Scotswoman in there.

What can I do for you? says Totemic Smith.

Ye fucking bastard!

The door open, wind abrading the three of them, Totemic Smith's spectacles stare at a man that doesnae seem to like him.

I don't think I know you.

And McPint comes in, his turnip nose and ear hair ablaze in his brusque squat body. For some reason he removes his cap. Totemic Smith shuts the door but not for wanting this man to stay.

McPint breathes in and out hard. He is in his most equilibrious state: fulmination. He throws his weight back and forth between his balls and his feet balls, he puts his hands in and out of his pockets. Totemic Smith sees he has an erection.

What gives you the right, says McPint.

He breathes harder, begins thrusting his fat fingers this way and that in the chill air.

What gives you the right?

Right to – eh, says Totemic Smith.

Oh yeah? What gives you the right tae come burstin in here? says China Pig.

What are ye talking about? says Totemic Smith. What do ye want?

I've seen your paintins, och aye, says McPint. It's an outrage, a public outrage. Ah saw them in the museum. Next the tapeworms where they belong. And let me tell you somethin, those tapeworms are fine solid men o the world compared wi you, ye fuckin bastard son of a bitch. Ah'd like to flay the skin aff yer miserable bones and shove it right up ye.

Look at that, says McPint, staring at the easel with fear. You've sold us oot, aye, ye've shown everybody our *weaknesses*. The English, aye – we've no defences left with bastards like you, corrupting us from inside. You ought tae be ashamed of yersel. What kind of a man *are* ye?

You can just bugger off right now, says China Pig, before I call the polis.

Aye, says McPint turning on her. I ken you. The dirty disgusting hoor wha's in all this bastard's paintins. Displayin yer ony-man's body fer a poond – I'll bet ye have tae pay *him* tae take yer claes aff! He's the only one who will. And I'll bet ye go with him too when his filthy work is done!

The way McPint speaks he is practically vomiting. He face is crimson and he staggers.

I ken you, I ken ye both, he keeps saying.

You've got no business here at all, says China
Pig. If he'll no throw you out, ah will!

Aye come on and try, ye bit hairie, says
McPint. It's bite yer tits off I will!

In a second China Pig is on him.

What do you know aboot paintin anyway? she
screams. What gives *you* the right tae come in
here like a bloody maniac, disturbin folk what's
tryin tae make a great statement, like Mr Smith?

Statement! yells McPint.

The truth, says China Pig, this man tells the
truth about all you back-alley buggers. *Ah* ken
you, ye rat-faced degenerate pervert! Oh aye!

He is strong, he hurts her, but she is quick:
the point of her battered hairie's high heel in
his nut sac. McPint groans and folds, a stain on
his trews.

It has come to Totemic Smith that he knows
this man, aye, from following his progress
through the city from the panorama. And from
the Taj Mahal. This is frightening to Totemic
Smith, to see this man who had already become
a subject, a squat determined drunk shoulder-
ing his way among the closes and temptations
of a corrupted Edinburgh . . . Totemic Smith
drops his cup and brushes.

Right you!

Totemic Smith pounds over to McPint and
picks him up like a dollop of pipe-clay. With
McPint struggling and cursing in his arms he
nods to China Pig who drags open the door.

I'll bloody kill you, I'll fucking kill the both of

you bloody buggers! screams McPint.

Totemic Smith lifts McPint high above him, McPint biting at his face. Totemic Smith heaves him backward and then throws him, a mile like, as if to throw him out of life, out of the world. McPint smashes into a stone wall in the old crazy alley. He mumbles and tries to get up, but can't, his arm will not work. He lies shuddering in a lot of blood, weeping.

What *right,* he says, what right do ye have to come inside my head, to show the world what I'm thinkin, what right to show the world what I'm *like*?

Jesus Christ, says China Pig.

Totemic Smith bars the door and switches off the lights except the heat lamp. In its dark red he lifts China Pig on to a stool, after slowly draping the bunting round her scratched shoulders and breasts.

They have a go. They both face the canvas, China Pig examining it in earnest now.

Done, he pats her hair, buttons his trousers, and rushes for the easel. He sets to work fast, hard, sweating, screwy. During the night McPint appears on the canvas, crouched, sailing through Scotland of the Night as he did from the door, over street-lamps, chippies, black brassières, newspapers, tooth-torn fleshes, and the intimater flanks of China Pig.

That's another ten pound ye owe me, she says as dawn comes.

RAIN EDINBURGH

Rain, ever. And as it falls you must fight your way up the streets, through an additional element, a grey spiritual aspic which seeps from the core of Edinburgh. Your shoes leaden like your heart. The end of the world's sorrowful aspirations impends, depends and dangles from the top of every Edinburgh rain-soaked hill.

On these days no one dares raise a proud remark or head, or curl a lip or nostril over the dull flat lands of Lothian or Fife. The thrilling glory of doom all Scotland rides on, the limits of life, are unavoidable on these heavy days. Like the infrequent bus they must be taken.

Pitch and roll of steamy bus interior. Jingle of bell, snarl of babe, spit of cat. Honk of adolescent. Outside the sky glowers and lowers it seems to the very roof of the bus.

Yet another ticket to be bought. On it a wee mannie, a mascot, thick thighs in a uniform. His face, through tired printing, a skull. Little death's head. Go By Bus, an unfortunate effect: through me the way.

Outside in the rain a vegetable stall. Cauliflowers glow dully, a pyramid of aubergines brags of strength and taste like cannonballs.

What's this, one's moving! Behind the veget-
ables, sitting on a low stool, the Pakistani – it's
his shop, his dark head an Urdu-speaking
aubergine. What a fright.

There are many who live in this weather all
the time. Trapped in it. One day they walked in
and never left. It's not so difficult . . . walking up
George Street in merciless winter, you enter the
rain world through its one-way door. Then you
live in it and it in you forever. You're mad,
you're a daftie.

You become a little mad daftie, haunting Rose
Street in the bit hours, hiding among memorials
in Princes Street Gardens. If you're a lucky
daftie you have a tiny sooty mass-murderer's
flat in Tollcross. Occasionally in the town you
want a cup of tea and the toilet. But is that your
due in Edinburgh?

Such a day. McPint and McX in a noisy café
near Queen Street. Having been thrown finally
out of the last most bend-the-law public house
they could lay their hands on. McX is silent.
McPint, drunk, also silent. Irascible and
flushed. McPint has got bashed up somehow, he
has bruises on his face and his right arm is in
a sling. Not something one speaks of. Despite
this, McPint had been hoping for a lunch-hour
punch-up and hadn't got it. Too many pound-
peelywallies, he said. His name for the young
men of St Andrew Square, they of the pallid
neckties.

McPint tried to drag McX across town to a

particularly disgusting all-day but McX refused. Although they got as wet in the space of two streets as they would have going the two miles. Bus or no. It rains in the buses as well, so you'll feel no relief in getting on one, taking up space, *wasting time.* The Curse of Little Death's Head.

McX has a letter full of rain from Siobhan. He keeps fingering it in the pocket of his sodden jacket. His fingers across that Highland handwriting. His cigarette sputters with wet. McPint's fag is wet too and stinks like cremation all over the café, which isn't inappropriate.

The tea is damp, it can hardly be drunk. It is grey, not brown, a tepid distillate of the city and the day. Actually, they're fit to be tied.

And across from them is a daftie. Young, young for a daftie, but well inside the everlasting rain-hoose of the head. It's hard enough seeing dafties in their rain-hooses on clear days, but to see one when you're on the threshold of the thing yourself, the heaviness outside – !

The daftie is making signs or drawings in a notebook. He's quite far gone for he's using a nib and pen and a bottle of ink. He's a pen-and-ink daftie. Spread about him at his table, other of his daftie things: a smooth rock, for caressing in doorways at night or at the absolute back of the top of a bus. A vegetable. A broken piece of enamel tile. A little box which might contain more daftie pen-points, or something else, awful. Or even more awful, nothing.

The daftie makes his calculations, or hiero-
glyphs, frequently looking up at people, includ-
ing McPint and McX. McPint can't take this. If
McX is paying attention to the daftie, he will do
two things. Part of McX will file away a few
observations on the daftie. McX thinks he is a
keen observer of men. However, what McX sees
in men is only himself, only those parts of them
which are like parts of him. He will put away a
few remarks on the daftie to be dragged out for
some pub woman of the future. And for a
moment McX will ruminate on the plight of puir
hameless dafties, and put this into his ongoing
neural lament for Scotland, which echoes in
him all night. Bong! Bong!

Fingering the damp letter from Siobhan, McX
also feels he or she may become a daftie. When
he has been angry with her, when the told-
what-to-do, the would-be modern Scotsman in
McX resents her, he has wanted to call her mad.
Despite his love for her he becomes frightened:
her hands.

Siobhan runs her hand across the cover of an
old book, her fingers flat on the worn leather.
Back and forth. Never has he seen someone
touch things so emotionally.

But this is not the miser's touch, not the
coveter's, not the child's. This is someone
taking to her heart only the oldest things, the
sickest creatures, the pieces of lace, the ancient
jewellery just about to leave the world. She
smooths their hair and whispers soothingly to

them on their death-beds.

With her small caress she removes an invisible dust which obscures the life of things, which she sees into. The movements of Siobhan's hands on an old thing are her fingers lightly wafting the water of a dark pool. She peers at the bottom.

At the time of stubble fields she brings in discarded corn stalks. For some hours arranges them in a pail by the fire, to give them a last home. To think of her tenderness toward some odd little thing she has found!

When she and McX looked in a jeweller's window, he would want to move on in a moment – jewels don't much interest a man trying to figure if he has enough money for the messages and a pint. But his squirming was often thwarted, then embarrassed and hushed by her soft staying, her gaze at not some fine piece but a dusty brooch whose tiger's-eye is nearly asleep, a ring worn thin, the agate become dull and stoury as the quarry of its birth. Or a little cameo whose face has finally tired of its unskilfulness, and prays for its next sale to be its last.

She has the same caress for leaves in autumn. When she places them in her leaf-press, surely she is pressing them to her heart. And she has touched her coat and boots that way when pulling them on to hasten outside at the cry of an injured bird.

She deserves to be loved for this, by anyone.

The blessing of her hand for the world's bereft objects, the homeless sneered-at things, all the victims of fashion and the cruel striving for profit. With slow strokes of her small tapered fingers she apologizes to these unbelongings for the treatment they got at the clumsy grasping hands of us all.

And God help McX for the times she has touched him that way. He knows it. But wasn't her love for him born of that other love? Around the corners of McX's eyes, you may see traces of his funeral. His corduroy jacket ever hanging dromedarically on him seemed to her his winding-sheet.

So this unique gentleness has angered McX. Taken on the face of things, judged the way everyone he knows would judge, Siobhan is a daftie. McX's temptation to dismiss her saddens him. His beard droops low, lower here in the café.

But *McPint.* McPint cannot stand this ferlie chap looking at him any longer, writing about him, perhaps caricaturing him in some daftie way in the wet book. McPint's soul bristles, he is iron filings, the daftie a red and yellow magnet.

Dafties know they irritate men like McPint, men who are on the rotten lower rungs of the ladder but believe with secret passion in the upper rungs, and want the whole to be fumigated. McPint is getting so hot so mad McX feels he's sitting next to a balefire. McX sinks through fathoms of silence, away from this café, away from McPint.

Now the rain grows furious, it seems the windows must break. Across Hanover Street a man falls. He can't get up, the wet furies of today's little doom are upon him, help, help.

In this worst of the storm the daftie begins to sing. And to pack up, he's attracted to the violence outside, it's so like what's going on in his strangely furnished head. Begins to pack up his mad-person things, his *tikis*, singing, still casting binocular looks at McPint.

When the weather between them can't get any worse and the daftie has shouldered his bag, he comes toward McPint. McX fears McPint will lose control, will burst, his fist creaks with clenching under the table.

I might say, says the daftie, *that those who fall upon the rock will merely be broken, but those on whom the rock falls will be crushed to powder.*

Stunned silence, storm continues in background. The daftie leers at McX and the struck-dumb McPint and whispers:

Powder!

again before shooting toward the door, daftie flaps flying in a queer side-to-side gait. Thunder a thousand times louder than the midday gun explodes outside and he's away, beckoned at by the man still lying across Hanover Street.

McPint burns at both ends, at a strange angle.

Did you hear that now? he says, did you *hear* that, about the rock?

This is an outrage for McPint.

Aye, says McX quietly, gazing into his awful tea.

Must be bloody off his fucking bloody rocker! says McPint.

If Siobhan were here, she would have jumped up and followed the daftie. She often gazes unthinking but without malice at the unfortunate. She loves to walk the burnt fields of their faces, to experience their always-winter. She fights to live in the realm not of tragedy, but of hardness. She loves struggle. All around her in childhood was that battle against the elements, the landlords, the banks.

Siobhan would give a fortune to spend a night among the poor folk of the Cowgate, and another never to ride in a sports car, or *be had* to dinner.

McX is thinking this. He slowly inserts his generally unsmoked cigarette into his cup of tea.

That's a waste of a good cigarette, that, scolds McPint.

Yes, says McX, I could have given it out to our friend before being crushed to powder.

McPint doesn't get it. He stares at McX, incredulous. This is not a laughing matter, the daftie's warning has gone deep with McPint. He has his own visions of being crushed to powder all right. But damned if the dafties don't deserve it before him!

I think you're a bloody bit daftie too, if you

want to know! he shouts at McX.

McX's grey eyes are full of rain, from the letter from Siobhan in the north. He is going to go off alone and think of her, go back to his encyclopaediac dream.

Well, I must get along, he says.

This further enrages McPint.

You're no going out in that, he says, why the bar'll be open in forty-five minutes!

Nevertheless, says McX.

He zips his plastic windcheater over the dromedary and abruptly leaves, mumbling Cheero the noo, not even stopping at the door for his usual blank reconnaissance of the atmospheres in and out.

In the rain world. McX squashes up to Princes Street. At the corner he closes his hand round a little one of air. Far away a mannie in an olive raincoat struggles up the Mound. Like a decrepit omnibus he labours, under some doom enforced by the cannons brooding on the ramparts of the Castle. Scotland yet. *Thanking you.*